A Mare's Tale

A Mare's Tale

by

Len Hall

J & J Publishing

Published by J & J Publishing

Published by J & J Publishing
Copyright©Len Hall

First published in Scotland in 2016 by
J & J Publishing
Ty Crwn, East Grange, Kinloss, Forres, Moray, IV36 2UD

Bespoke publishing
Typeset by J & J Publishing
Design by J & J Publishing 01343 850 123

Jacket design by Harvey Pettit
harveypettit@gmail.com

Proofread and edited by Susan Kemp
holorose@hotmail.com

Printed in the UK by
4edge Ltd
7a Eldon Way, Eldon Way Industrial Estate, Hockley, Essex, SS5 4AD

ISBN: 978-0-9543891-9-2

Acknowledgements

Although I have written quite a number of articles for various newspapers and magazines this is the first book I have attempted to write. I am very grateful to Jacqui Jones, J & J Publishing, based in Forres who taught me all I now know about publishing. She has done this with patience and good humour and this I appreciate very much.

I also acknowledge the help I have had from several of my carer girls (ladies) who guided me over many difficulties with my vintage computer (and vintage me!).

But most of all my thanks are to Ernie Hay who never failed to keep me right and take me out for a meal or just afternoon tea because I am not allowed to drive now (and not for <u>that</u> reason), just my age!

Lastly, my thanks to Susan Drysdale for showing me how to use two hands to type with and Sheena, my daughter, who jogged my failing memory with place names, events and so on and many others who have helped in various ways.

Onye wye 'ats fit freens are for, noo, g'wan read an' enjoy A Mare's Tale!

One of the author's favourite Doric poems by Chares Murray

It wasna his wyte he was beddit sae late
An' him wi' sae muckle to dee,
He'd the rabbits to feed an' the fulpie to kame
An' the hens to hish into the ree;

The mason's mear syne he set up in the closs
An' coupit the ladle fu' keen,
An' roon the ruck foun's wi' the lave o' the loons
Played "Takie" by licht o' the meen.

Syne he rypit his pooches an' coontit his bools,
The reed-cheekit pitcher an' a',
Took the yirlin's fower eggs fae his bonnet, an' fegs,
When gorbell't they're fykie to blaw ;

But furth cam' his mither an' cried on him in,
Tho' sairly he priggit o' wait –
"The'll be nae wird o' this in the mornin', my laad" –
But it wasna his wyte he was late.

"Och hey ! " an' "Och hum ! " he was raxin himsel'
An' rubbin' his een when he raise,
An' faur was his bonnet, an' faur was his beets
An' fa had been touchin' his claes?

Ach ! his porritch was caul', they'd forgotten the saut,
There was owre muckle meal on the tap.
Was this a' the buttermilk, faur was his speen,
An' fa had been bitin' his bap?

His pints wasna tied, an' the backs o' his lugs
Nott some sma' attention as weel –
But it wasna as gin it was Sabbath, ye ken,
An' onything does for the squeel.

Excerpt from 'It Wisn'a his Wyte' in Doric by Charles Murray

Cullokie, Scotland
1928

Chapter 1
Andrew teams up with Jeannie

Andrew Sproat was a familiar sight in Cullokie and the surrounding area, with his somewhat odd-looking horse-drawn cart, which had bonny gig wheels and two low slung churns at the rear. Nobody passed by without a cheery wave and people set their clocks by Andrew.

Andrew worked for a farmer known in the area as Blairmoss, the same name as his farm, in accordance with local custom. Andrew had done Blairmoss's milk round for the past ten years, ever since he was discharged from the army after his thigh was shattered by a German machine-gun bullet during one of those crazy attacks over no-man's land in broad daylight at the terrible Battle of Passchendaele, fought in July 1917. He still had his leg, a little bit of pension and a lot of pain but he could still walk and work. Before he went away with the Territorial Army (better known as the Terriers) he had been second horseman at the Mains of Blairmoss Farm, though he could never cope with a day's ploughing now. Blairmoss, however, had a notion to start a milk round serving the expanding Cullokie and other small towns along the Moray coast and he tried out Andrew to see if he could manage. He got a local joiner to strengthen a gig and to adapt it with a low-level shelf at the back end to accommodate a pair of milk churns and a platform for Andrew to stand on. It was nearly at ground level so he had no climbing to do. Andrew got on fine with his customers and soon built up a healthy round. Most folk, aware of his disability, helped Andrew to avoid taxing his leg too much by coming out to the cart with their pails for him to ladle out their milk. Blaikie, the cross-bred garron that Blairmoss had bought especially for the milk round, very soon was more familiar with the round than Andrew and he knew when there would be an apple, a sugar lump or a sweetie.

Day in, day out, year in, year out, Andrew and Blaikie did their round; summer and winter, wet or dry and it seemed that they would go on forever. But one day, halfway through the round, Blaikie stumbled, a most unusual thing for him. It was just a few faltering steps but it was enough for Andrew to take his head and lead him through the rest of the round. When he had stabled, groomed and fed him that afternoon, Andrew noticed that his head was down and he gave him a handful of cake and threw a blanket over his back. After he had his tea, he said to his wife that he was going down to the stable to see how the horse was. It seemed that Blaikie was waiting for him to come back down for as soon as Andrew came alongside him in his stall, Blaikie muzzled him, gave a whinny, dropped on to his knees very gently and died.

THE NEXT day Blairmoss and Andrew did the round with a box cart, with Andrew driving as well as dispensing the milk. Great were the lamentations at the passing of old Blaikie. As soon as the round was finished, Blairmoss and Andrew visited the mart and before the night was out there was a new shelt in Blaikie's stall. Now if old Blaikie had a lot of character, his replacement had plenty of good looks and style. Much lighter in body and standing several hands higher than Blaikie, the new mare had a sleek, smooth, chestnut coat with a black mane and a look of an Arab in her. She was broken in and used to town work, according to her vendor, but used to long unbroken runs. She would have to get used to 'stop and start' type of work.

The first day on the round was sheer hell for Andrew, the new horse and the customers. Everybody missed Blaikie but a keen interest was taken in his replacement. Her name? To tell the truth, in the hurry and excitement of buying her, her name had never been mentioned so a new one had to be found. Many suggestions were offered and as Andrew wondered how to choose, he had a great idea. The next day he wrote everybody's suggestion for a name on a slip of paper and popped it into a bank bag he carried on his cart for keeping change. One of his last customers on his round was old Jeannie McRae, nearly ninety, but with a mind as sharp as a nineteen year-old. She was liked by everybody along the coast but reckoned to be a very fly body when it came to getting her own way about anything. Andrew asked Jeannie to put her choice of name into the bag and then draw out what was to be the shelt's new name. Out came the name Andredopholus and Jeannie was delighted, for that was the name she had put in. Apparently, many years ago her brother was home from Australia and he persuaded her to put a pound on a horse called Andredopholus in the Grand National; the only bet she ever made in her whole life. The horse won and Jeannie got over £50 back!

Now some of the folk who knew her, wondered if it was more than just coincidence that Jeannie had palmed her own entry and then drawn it out again to make sure that her chosen name was given to the new milk cart horse.

"The auld besom wid be fly enough," said some.

Others said, "There's nae lengths she widn'a gang tae get her ain wye!"

At all events Andrew's shelt could never have a long fancy name like that and it could not be abbreviated, for it could sound like Andrew. So, Andrew himself made the decision, heartily approved of all round, and called his horse Jeannie.

Jeannie quickly became a favourite on the round, even more than old Blaikie had been. There was something in the way she held herself; she was dignified, almost majestic in her stance. At the end of her day's work, after her daily apple and half a dozen sugar lumps from her master, she took to trotting home with so smooth a gait that never a drop of milk was spilt on Andrew's cart. Andrew was proud of her and enjoyed the admiring glances his rig got as they went about their business.

ONE DAY, going down the main street of Cullokie, Andrew was aware of a huge fancy car standing with its engine running alongside Para Finnie's petrol pump at the edge of the pavement. Para himself was at the hand-operated pump, working hard at the handle, filling up the sight glass and then discharging it into the car's cavernous petrol tank. As Jeannie stopped to let Mrs Finnie get her milk, Para came round to the driver's door and said to the leather-clad and bonneted man at the wheel, "Would you mind shutting off your engine, Sir. It's burning up the petrol quicker than I can put it in!"

Switching the engine off, the gent got out of the car, leaned on the extensive bonnet and said to Andrew, "That's a fine looking bit of horseflesh you have there, my good man."

Andrew had hardly ever been spoken to in such an accent since his army days and he almost instinctively drew himself up to attention as he voiced his agreement. As the conversation developed, the war and Andrew's wound were discussed and it transpired that the gent was Colonel Marsh MC, late of the Scots Greys, and now building up a business as a racehorse trainer at Newmarket. He had been in the area of Cullokie on military and police business and had been paying a rather sad visit to the family of a wartime friend, the laird of a big estate in the area who had been killed on active service early in the war.

When the discussion came back to the mare, Andrew had to confess that he knew nothing of her breeding or of her background and, as far as he knew, neither did his boss who owned her. Certainly the Colonel was very interested in Jeannie and suggested that he would like to have a word with Blairmoss and drove off.

When Andrew got back to Blairmoss with Jeannie, he was surprised to see Colonel Marsh standing with his boss waiting for him. A riding saddle was found and put on Jeannie and the Colonel, dressed as he was in his leather coat, mounted and took Jeannie down the farm road. It was obvious that Jeannie was back in her natural element, with a skilful rider on her back and no cart behind. Turning, they came back up the road at the gallop, jumped clean over the fence and away, as if on wings, across the ley park. Blairmoss and Andrew watched in amazement and when the Colonel and Jeannie eventually drew up panting at the stable, not a word was said as Andrew took a steaming Jeannie into the stable for a rub down.

It was later that night when Blairmoss came to Andrew's door to tell him what had transpired. Over a glass of the good stuff, Blairmoss told Andrew that Colonel Marsh had been very impressed with Jeannie and was convinced that she had some, perhaps a lot, of very good blood in her and that she had the potential to become a racing horse. He wanted to buy her and had offered a very good price but Blairmoss wanted time to think on such a deal. That afternoon's performance had made quite an impression on him and although the price the Colonel had offered was one he could hardly refuse, he was now interested in how an animal of that quality came to be on the market as a jobbing carthorse.

Chapter 2
Andrew arrives in Suffolk

Over the next few weeks there was a lengthy exchange of correspondence between Blairmoss and the Colonel, the outcome being that Jeannie would stay at Blairmoss for the next few months to be looked after by Andrew but that she would stop working on the milk round. Instead, she was to be regularly exercised as a riding horse until the Colonel came back from an overseas trip to which he was committed.

As part of the deal with the Colonel, the milk round would be done with a small ex-army truck instead of the horse float. Andrew thought of the advantages of doing his job as a lorry driver, doing the round in a shorter time and so on, but he would have no companionship with a petrol engine and it would not eat sweeties and apples like a horse. On the other hand, he would learn to drive and maybe have a car of his own! He thought it would please his wife Kirsty that he could drive her into Elgin or Keith to do a bit of shopping or go to the pictures.

The plan went ahead and Andrew soon learned to drive but he had no heart for his job without his horse. The truck never learned which house to stop at and the camaraderie between the customers and Andrew rapidly disappeared. Worse than that, Andrew's leg gave him considerable pain. Stepping up a few inches on to the low platform at the rear of the float was one thing but having to clamber down and climb up again to the driving seat at every stop was another. However, having the motor shortened the time for the round and he was able to devote more time to Jeannie.

Since being wounded he had hardly been on a horse's back but he had found that on Jeannie's back his damaged leg was no impediment and he grew to feel very much at home on horseback. Before long, he was confident enough to jump Jeannie and the pair of them became well known far and wide as they roamed the countryside; Jeannie for her grace and Andrew for his stiff-legged style in the saddle.

When the Colonel returned, there was another meeting to decide Jeannie's future and this time Andrew was invited to attend. Andrew showed Jeannie's paces before they got down to business and the Colonel was very pleased with what he had seen and heard. Andrew explained the difficulty he was having with his leg in the lorry and that he would have to give up his job as roundsman.

As the various possibilities were examined it became clear to Andrew that since the Colonel was determined to have the horse and Blairmoss was being tempted by the price, his future looked uncertain. In the end it was agreed that Jeannie would go to the Colonel's stables at Newmarket in Suffolk, the home of British horse racing and that Andrew would be found a lighter job after he had trained a new man to the milk round.

JEANNIE'S DEPARTURE was a sad event for everyone at Blairmoss and the surrounding area. The news that she had been spotted as a racehorse soon got round and before long rumour had it that she was a likely future Ascot winner! But for Andrew it was an especially sad day, losing the horse had been more like losing a pal than a servant. His new job, though an easy one, seldom brought him into contact with horses and he had started to wonder about making a new start somewhere else when he got a message that Blairmoss wanted to have a word with him that evening. He went with some trepidation, fearing in a way that this was the end of the road, for he knew that his new job had been more or less made especially for him. He need never have worried for he was taken into the parlour and on a table in front of the fire was a bottle of whisky, two glasses, a letter and a smile on Blairmoss's face.

The glasses charged, the pleasantries over, Blairmoss asked Andrew if he had ever been to Suffolk. Andrew had been on a despatch-rider course at Cambridge during the war and he recalled the countryside around there being rather flat and featureless but remembered little else about it.

"How would you like to go to Newmarket to look after Jeannie and help with the other horses at the Colonel's stables?" said Blairmoss.

Andrew could hardly believe what he was hearing – an ordinary, crippled man being invited to go to a place where horses were in the blood of the locals to look after an erstwhile carthorse!

He gathered from Blairmoss that the letter explained how Jeannie had made quite an impression on the racing fraternity and the Colonel's early belief that there was top-class blood there had been confirmed. The Colonel's research had shown that early in the war when horses were being commandeered wholesale for service in France, there had been a fiddle in the paperwork and Jeannie had been branded in place of a working cob from Skegness. A civilian official in the Army Veterinary Corps had made quite a bit of illicit money for himself by swapping papers with the connivance of various horse dealers before he was detected. A minor aristocrat, a serving officer, had been paid an amount the equivalent of a working horse for his exceptionally well-bred racehorse and because he was at the front, and absent during the deal, the fraud had gone undetected. Moreover, the civilian official had destroyed all the records of the transactions when he realised that he was about to be arrested.

When demobilisation of commandeered horses took place, the authorities, rather than be embarrassed by having to reveal what had taken place, allowed the racehorse to be returned to the dealer from whom the workhorse had originally been commissioned. In the confusion of the time, the valuable racehorse was sold into the market as a hack, to be sold on again until it finally came to Blairmoss.

The Colonel had eventually got a lead to the story from a demobilised groom who had been in the Veterinary Corps and who had picked up a whisper of the deception. He knew the name of the civilian official who had masterminded the fraud. This man was still in prison but when the Colonel visited him there, he remembered the name of the original owner who had been swindled. Further enquiries revealed that he had not survived the war and his family were no longer involved or interested in horses. By means of blood tests, the bloodstock authorities had been persuaded to recognise the true blood lines of the racehorse and Jeannie had been admitted to the records in her own right.

After her move from Blairmoss to Newmarket, Jeannie had simply failed to settle. Despite the efforts of the trainer and his staff, she had lost condition and seemed to have lost her zest for living. As her condition deteriorated, the Colonel made up his mind that either Jeannie had to go back to Scotland or her old master, Andrew, had to come down to care for her, so he wrote the letter which was to dramatically change Andrew's life.

Blairmoss and Andrew sat and debated the situation until the bottle of whisky was well down. Although he was appreciative of the way his boss had created a job for him, he was not happy because he had lost all contact with the world of horses and people. There was not much challenge in his new job, perhaps it was too easy and he missed the daily contact and chaff with his customers. The thought of teaming up with his old friend Jeannie, albeit in an entirely different environment and the very good offer of a house and good wages, was enough to make up his mind. Confident that his wife would also be happy with the move, Andrew said he would go and that he would be in Suffolk within the week.

Chapter 3
Life at the stables

It was a late winter's afternoon and Andrew had just arrived from Scotland, in advance of his family. The driver – the Colonel's chauffeur, who had met him at Cambridge station – said that he had been instructed to take him straight to where Jeannie was stabled.

Andrew entered the stable, which he had been told held Jeannie. When he saw her, his heart sank and he realised that the urgency of the Colonel's call to him was genuine and justified. Jeannie was but a shadow of her former self. In the month or so she had been at Colonel Marsh's stables she had gone steadily downhill, barely eating and becoming completely lethargic. Several vets had examined her and cleared her of possible causes such as grass sickness, growths or bowel disorders and Mr Snodgrass, the senior vet in the practice, had pronounced that she was pining, either for someone, some place, some routine, or possibly all three.

Kneeling beside Jeannie on the ample straw bed, stroking Jeannie's ears and speaking gently to her was a motherly figure, her hair showing beneath a sloppy felt hat hanging on by its chinstrap. She was clad in jodhpurs and pullover of a style, which indicated that they were intended for work and not show. Andrew knelt beside her and Jeannie and said softly,

"Aye, Aye Jeannie, fit's 'is ah've bin hearin' aboot ye?"

The effect was electric – Jeannie's head came up and she made an attempt at a whinny, and then tried to stand up. Andrew eased her back down and she lay there content, her eyes never straying from Andrew's face as he patted her neck and rubbed her muzzle.

It was warm and cosy in the stall, the soft light of the stable lantern bathed the scene in a cosy glow and the silence was broken only by the hissing of the lamp, the horse's breathing and the soft words of encouragement and comfort, which Andrew spoke to the now relaxed mare. Only then did Andrew become really aware of the presence of the lady who had obviously been trying in vain to console Jeannie and he felt a strange warmth towards her. His leg cramped, he attempted to stand up but Jeannie was having none of it and made another attempt to get to her feet. The lady also tried to stand but stumbled and in the confusion Jeannie was on her feet, whinnying and muzzling the pair on the floor, Andrew sitting on the straw with the lady leaning backwards against his chest. For a moment they sat there relaxed, then realised that perhaps they shouldn't be and made a move to get up but their eyes met and they relaxed again, comfortable in their closeness and enjoying it. Though utter strangers until a few minutes ago, a strong bond was linking them so they sat, enjoying the warmth, the masculine and feminine smells of each other, watching Jeannie tearing hay from the rack and munching contentedly, a totally changed animal.

The lady spoke for the first time. "Never before have I seen such a thing, a horse we had given up for dead and one sniff and sight of you and she comes alive again – absolutely bloody marvellous."

She imperceptibly snuggled closer to Andrew and her head went back on to his shoulder so that she could look up into his eyes and she was aware of the pressure on her thigh as Andrew moved a little to allow his manhood to achieve its full strength. Andrew's mind was in a whirl. He had left his wife many hundreds of miles away in Scotland just a few hours ago and here he was, delighted to see Jeannie respond to his presence but delirious that he was lying in the fresh straw bed in a warm stable, alone with a woman who obviously needed him and he not averse to fulfilling her. It flashed through his mind that he hadn't been in such a situation since the time when he had been on sentry duty on a farm in France during the war, when an eighteen year-old mademoiselle had sidled up to him and suggested she could do him a favour for a wad of francs. He had no qualms of conscience then; it was a business deal born of mutual necessity.

But this was different. He was older and should have been wiser but the pressure in his groins was overcoming his conscience. His arms tightened about her and in return her hands moved down and sought his fly buttons. One touch there and Andrew moved his hands to find her fastenings. But she had already started to loosen her jodhpurs and her mouth moved up to meet Andrew's trembling lips. They rolled over and with the smoothness of two experienced lovers they were as one. It was soon over and they lay there in the straw bed, panting, satisfied and pleased with themselves.

Jeannie, meantime, was ignoring the pair of them, content with a full belly and with the certainty that she was once more in her master's care. A movement by Jeannie made the pair on the stable floor remember their compromising state and they got up to sort themselves out. Only then did they have the opportunity to see one another properly and what they saw mutually pleased them. Andrew, six feet tall, aged thirty-five and of strong build, was a pleasing bit of manhood as he coyly looked at the woman of more than forty, of moderate height and with a figure kept trim by an active life. No conversation had passed between them and she said simply, "I'm Marion and you'll be Andrew from Scotland. Cedric, you met him – he's the one who brought you from the station – had to go and take one of the Colonel's guests to the train immediately after he had brought you here. He knew you would want to see Jeannie as soon as you arrived and he asked me to wait for you and take you to your digs."

The thought passed through Andrew's mind as to whether she had understood this to mean make herself available to him but he decided that the answer was 'no', so he merely thanked her and they walked in silence across the dark stable courtyard and through an archway surmounted by a clock tower. Andrew saw the lights of a quite large two-storey house ahead and asked if that was the Colonel's home – a question which brought a laugh from Marion.

"No, no, that's Peter the head stable boy's house and that's where you'll be lodged until your family arrive. You'll be very comfortable and well looked after there. The Colonel's house is just a little bit bigger!"

As they walked to the house they were not physically close but there was a strong feeling between them – both seemed aware of it but when they arrived at Peter's house Marion made the briefest of polite introductions to the maid who opened the door and quickly disappeared into the night almost before Andrew could thank her.

CEDRIC HAD delivered Andrew's valise and other gear and he found his belongings already up in his room when he was taken up to it. It was large, with a partly coombed ceiling and simply, but pleasantly, furnished. He opened the softly patterned curtains and looked out to the distant lights of the stable courtyard, the place where his immediate future lay, then closed them and lay down on his bed. He clasped his hands behind his head and thought over the events of the day. He had risen early and said a fond farewell to his wife and bairns before Blairmoss called to take him to catch the Aberdeen train for his long train journey to Cambridge. He had to change trains at Edinburgh, Peterborough and Ely before his joyous and meaningful reunion with Jeannie. The enjoyable session with this strange, but fascinating, woman called Marion had been unexpected; it had been quite a day! As he washed and rather wearily prepared for bed, his mind kept coming back to her – who was she? What was her involvement in the stables? What was her involvement with the Colonel and Jeannie? The whys and wherefores of that brief period in the stable filled his mind as he drifted off to sleep. His last thoughts were that however fascinating she was, he had to go very, very warily in that direction.

ANDREW WAS wakened at seven by the maid placing a mug of steaming tea by his bedside and telling him, with Master Peter's compliments, that Colonel Marsh would call for him at nine o'clock. Adding in her Suffolk way of speech, "And if you don't mind me making so bold as to be saying it, when the Colonel says nine o'clock he means nine o'clock and he be none too pleased if he be kept awaiting. Begging your pardon, Sir, but I'll have breakfast on the table at eight and I hope you can manage two eggs with your ham."

"This is the life," thought Andrew as he washed, shaved and put on his best working tweed suit, ready for whatever the day might bring. He had in mind to step over to the stables to see Jeannie before the appointed breakfast time but decided that he had better not take any initiatives until he had decided who was who and what was what. At eight precisely he went into the kitchen to find his host, and his host's family, waiting to welcome him. After introductions all round and enquiring how he liked his room and how well he had slept, the serious business of eating breakfast and discussing the day ahead – obviously a very important part of the household routine – began in earnest.

The children's day at school was discussed, household matters vented and Peter's plans for the day explained in as far as they affected the household. Andrew, at first a silent observer, was impressed by the way Peter unobtrusively handled things while letting his wife make the decisions when they were called for. Andrew decided he was a past master at delegation. When Peter's children had gone off to school they briefed Andrew on the domestic matters as they affected him, meal times and so on. When Peter's wife, Joan, had left to attend her chores Peter outlined in general terms what he thought Colonel Marsh had in mind for the development of the estate and Jeannie's part in his plans. It was left that the Colonel would explain his plans to Andrew later in the morning and that the three of them would have their morning cup of tea in the Hall, after which Peter would take Andrew on a tour of the whole estate.

ON THE dot of nine, there was a toot on a car horn and Andrew stepped out to meet his new boss. He was out of his bonny Bentley and greeted Andrew warmly, as two old friends rather than employer and employee, and invited Andrew to climb aboard for the short trip to the stables. Andrew told him that part of last night's events, which concerned Jeannie and Colonel Marsh was over the moon when he saw the change in her. With Andrew present she made a fuss of the Colonel and showed no signs of the lethargy that had caused so much worry in the stable. He called together those of the stable staff who were around and after introducing Andrew asked that Jeannie and his own hunter be saddled. As Andrew mounted, he felt a tremor of delight rippling along Jeannie's back and soon they were out under the clock tower and ambling along the sandy path towards the exercise area. Without a word being said it was understood that Jeannie would have to be exercised very gently and the Colonel had some difficulty in retraining his hunter, who was all set for a fierce gallop.

As they walked gently along Colonel Marsh talked. "My training stable venture is making some headway and the hard work of the first few years since my return from the war is beginning to pay off. You will only have met West, my head stable lad, and a few of the stable staff, but I have arranged for West to take you round the estate and introduce you more widely. I hope you will like what you find and agree with me that we have here the nucleus of a successful rearing, training and racing business. Peter West has been a pillar of strength to me and has managed the stables to perfection." He hesitated briefly before continuing, "But now I need what you might call a general manager, someone to oversee the whole operation, to act as my sergeant major, so to speak, and I would like you to take on that job."

Andrew was dumbstruck. He had felt like this only once before and that was when his sergeant had called him out from the squad in 1914 and made him a lance corporal. "You will not look at me in that tone of voice laddie, I say you will be corporal and corporal you will be! And you had better be a damned good one or I'll know the reason why. Now fall out and collect your squad and try, nay succeed, in smartening them up, for by God they need it. DISMISS."

They rode in silence for a few minutes before Andrew blurted out, "Begging your pardon, Sir, but why do you not give this job to Peter West, a man you know and trust and who has already proved himself. I am very honoured to be asked, Sir, but …".

His protest faded on his lips as Colonel Marsh raised his hand, commanding silence.

"Think it over, Sproat, and we will talk more of it at nine tomorrow morning. Now we will ride to the Hall for a cup of tea and I will hand you over to Peter. But think on; I, in my turn, have given this a great deal of intense thought and have made up my mind. Your place is here."

DURING THIS last exchange, for a few minutes, time slipped back many years and Andrew was once more a sergeant planning a sortie against the enemy lines with his Commanding Officer (CO). He unthinkingly sat more upright in his saddle and "Sir!" crept back into his vocabulary; he had seldom used the word since the war.

Andrew and the Colonel talked of other things until they dismounted in the rear courtyard of the Hall, where two lads took charge of the horses.

"Walk, not ride those horses back to the stables," said the Colonel, "and if you think you can handle her, you can take mine for a hard ride after you have stabled Jeannie and made her comfortable."

The Colonel was once again the benign laird, treating his underlings with feeling and firmness as they joined Peter West for their 'morning' in the kitchen, their cup livened with a drop from his generous hip flask. Then, with a crisp, "Till nine tomorrow then, Sproat, enjoy your tour," he left them.

The rest of the day passed in a whirl for Andrew; meeting people, seeing things and generally realising that life in Suffolk was very different from the life he had left in Scotland. Peter had a converted army staff car for getting round the estate, reasonably comfortable, seating for two and a small truck body behind for transporting the many odds and ends needed in running stables and they talked a lot about the estate, the job and themselves. It was not till late afternoon that they returned home and Andrew had an hour to himself before their evening meal.

He thought to himself that he had met many nice people, seen a most interesting estate cum business enterprise and had been propositioned by his boss to take on a job, which he wondered if he could handle. Yesterday had been a hectic day and this one looked as if it, too, was going to be memorable. His thoughts went back to Cullokie, to his wife and family and other folk he had left behind. Left behind, he thought, or was it abandoned? True, he had thought little of them but there had been hardly a minute to think and yet he had thought a lot about the mysterious woman of his first night – she kept coming into his mind as he thought over his future. Who was she and where, if at all, did she fit into the scene of the estate he had been shown. An estate thriving against the trend of the time, when many were failing and falling into neglect, an estate being led by a man with ideas and apparently the ability to carry them out, an estate to which he had been invited to commit his future?

Soon he was called to join Peter and his family for their evening meal which, to mark his arrival, was to be a bit special and to be in the dining room although it was only Wednesday and not Christmas Day! When he entered the simple but elegant room his heart thumped when he saw Marion sitting at the table with the rest of the family, looking cool, calm, composed as well as radiant in a simple velvet dress. Their eyes met and a simple message was exchanged in a single look saying, "What happened is between us – we say nothing."

As he took his place at the table opposite Marion, Peter said to Andrew, "Of course you met Marion when you arrived last night – she kindly sat with Jeannie until you arrived. Marion is my sister-in-law, Joan's sister, she lives in one of the coachmen's houses beside the clock tower. Her husband was the Colonel's Adjutant until he was killed when he drove over a landmine in the last week of the war. She now plays a most important part in the estate enterprise as the Colonel's secretary and personal assistant. You'll be seeing a lot of each other."

The phrase struck Andrew as both innocent and significant and, by the quick look exchanged between them, so did Marion!

The meal which followed was indeed special – home-made onion soup, followed by the traditional English roast beef, Yorkshire pudding, potatoes done to a flowery turn, peas, cauliflower cheese and gravy. Andrew had a prodigious appetite and did full justice to Joan's fine cooking and was even able to manage a second helping of the trifle, which Joan said had been Marion's contribution to the meal. It was odd, mused Andrew to himself. Everything they had eaten was delicious but that trifle beat all!

As they ate they talked and Andrew found out all about life at Chinglebrook School, which the West children attended and to which Andrew's bairns would go. Peter and Joan's boys, Robert and Alfred, thought their teacher, Miss Protheringay was a dear but the headmaster, Mr Cramond, was a terrible tyrant and used the belt for any breach of discipline. Listening to them prattling on, Andrew suspected that they really admired Mr Cramond and generally believed that he punished them only when they deserved it. Apparently he encouraged all of his pupils to take an interest in the world about them and made his staff organise outings and make the pupils keep records of what they had seen and done. Andrew liked what he heard about the school.

When the children had gone off to bed and the remains of the meal were cleared away, Andrew went to his room and brought down a bottle of eighteen-year-old Glen Cullokie malt whisky and was pleased that Peter, Joan and Marion appreciated a drop of the good cratur. Peter in particular appeared to be especially fond of a fine malt and when Joan asked if that was the best whisky, Andrew had to offer the simple but true reply, "But all whiskies are good – it's just that some are better than others!"

A VERY pleasant evening followed and under the influence of the good stuff Andrew got to know something of the histories of his new-found friends. He had already decided that he liked Peter and felt less worried about the job he had been offered when he learned Peter's story and his philosophy on life.

Peter West had been head stable lad with Colonel Marsh since he started the stable venture shortly after the war. The description 'lad' was of bit of a misnomer, for Peter was well in his late forties and fitted the description of 'lad' only in build, being five-feet-three-inches in height and slightly built with it. Despite being rather older than usual he had served in the Royal Flying Corps during the war as an air observer and bomber – perhaps his slight weight was an advantage in that a greater weight of bombs could be carried! Despite having landed twice behind the enemy lines due to engine failure, he had survived the war without injury and, when he found employment with Colonel Marsh, resumed his pre-war job as stable lad. People often asked him why he had never ridden as a jockey, being of the right size, but he always replied that he did not have the truly competitive spirit required. Peter would say, "Horses are my life and no man can be happier than I am when astride a handsome horse going for all its worth along a beach or over turf, with the wind whistling in your ears to accompany the thundering of the hooves. But it is only a pleasure if it is done for joy and not just to beat another noble horse. As a stable lad, I get the pleasure of riding fine horses without having to compete. Ah yes, I train them to run fast and give of their best but it is left to someone else to do the winning and that suits me just fine."

Peter explained all this as the four of them sat round a roaring log fire in the West's sitting room. He went on to say that here he had a good job with enough responsibility to satisfy without taxing him. He, Joan, Robert and Alfred lived comfortably in a nice house in a pleasant situation and the children had a good school and were doing quite well; it was quite likely that when the children grew up a bit Joan would get a job teaching in the school. Joan's origins were in Cheshire and she had met and married Peter when he was stationed at the aerodrome at Sealand in Flintshire, when he was being trained as an air observer. On a visit to Peter's family, she had fallen completely for the flat lands around Cambridge and was very happy with her life.

WHEN IT came to Andrew's turn, he had a fairly simple story to tell – brought up in the north-east of Scotland, the son of a crofter, he received a rigid but sound grounding in the three R's from a typical 'dominie' of the period – "If ye wint tae work, laddie, I'll gie ye a' the help I can but if ye dinna want tae learn, I canna dee onything for ye!"

Andrew had wanted to work but times were hard and money was scarce so he had to leave his schooling at fourteen and work on a farm ("tak a fee" as they said) and he worked at the Mains of Blairmoss, rising to be second horseman but then the war came. Like most other lads of the period he had enlisted in the Territorial Army, in the 5/7th Gordon Highlanders. When his audience expressed mild surprise at the enthusiasm shown by the men of the north-east farming community to enlist and train to fight, he had some difficulty in explaining the reasons. He thought that the extra money played a part, that and the annual camp and the glamour of the kit uniform. But in his opinion it was to provide a break from the sheer monotony of their lives – the constant grind of long hours, hard work, unimaginative diet and unrelenting poverty. Andrew recalled the pleasure of a week's camp at Barrybuddon. Bleak though it was, he remembered it to be enjoyable because of the company of other men sharing the discomforts of living under canvas, the ample and varied food, even if cooked by army cooks, and because it was a chance to get paid while seeing a little of another world. So, when the war came, these same men marched cheerfully to face to horrors of war, thinking that it would just be an extended camp and sadly many of them never lived long enough to have a chance to regret it.

Andrew rose to the rank of sergeant and was destined to be promoted to Regimental Sergeant Major of the Battalion when the bullet struck. He finished the war behind a desk, hating every minute of it but being wise enough to learn as much as he could of administration.

He had married Kirsty, a lass from his own station in life, when on leave from France and they had two children, both boys, Alex aged eleven and Jamie, who was thirteen. He had pondered hard about moving to town after the war, as many of his friends did, but Kirsty was not keen and when he got the chance of the milk round, he stayed on in Cullokie. His love of horses had been there since his youth, when he found that he 'had a way with them', even before he received the mystic 'horseman's grip and word' at a dreadful ceremony in the stable at Cullokie two years before the war.

Marion added little about herself to what Peter had previously told Andrew, simply that she had been married during the war to a Scots Grey Officer who was killed just as the war ended. She said that she had spent quite some time in the Channel Isles before the war and that accounted for the slight trace of an accent, which folks said she had. Peter and his wife agreed with Andrew that they had not detected any foreignness in her speech and they all laughed it off.

Andrew was intrigued with this woman and as the evening wore on he found himself wanting to know more about her but was aware that she was not going to lift the flimsy curtain of mystery with which she had surrounded herself. But Andrew thought to himself, "Come time lassie, come time, you'll tell me all."

Peter and Andrew took the dogs out to walk Marion home.

It was a fine winter's night and as they walked under the canopy of clear stars, Andrew thought about his family at home, resting under the same sky but he also thought that one day Marion would tell him all and – somewhat shamefully – he realised that he was looking forward to it.

Chapter 4
Andrew takes on responsibility

Next day followed the same pattern, with another ham and egg breakfast and the toot of the Colonel's car horn at nine precisely. In the car Colonel Marsh was brief to the point of bluntness. "I hope you've made up your mind on my proposition. Will you take on the job?"

Andrew replied, "Yes," just as briefly and Colonel Marsh wasted no time, "Right we will go and look at the house I have in mind for you and your family – I hope you will find it satisfactory." In a few moments they stopped outside a delightful cottage, standing by itself on a slight rise in front of a small beech wood facing up to the morning sun.

"Do you think this will do?" he said, as they walked up to the front door through a garden that, if looking rather sad in its winter neglect, gave the impression that it would respond well to loving care.

Inside, Andrew liked what he saw and could hardly believe that he was being offered this lovely house as his home. He had no doubt in his mind that Kirsty would be equally thrilled with it. He had already had discussions with Peter about how the children would get to school – both now and when they were ready for senior school – and he saw no difficulties so he accepted the house there and then, to the Colonel's pleasure. As they drove the half-mile or so back to the stables the discussion switched to Jeannie's future.

"No doubt you'll have guessed, Andrew, that I have set my heart on Jeannie winning Ascot for us. You may well think that it is over-ambitious, maybe even arrogant, of me to even think that a former milk-cart horse, with a simple name like Jeannie, could do such a thing but my intuition and hunches about that horse have been correct from the moment I first saw her up in Scotland. Now you, Peter, Marion and I are going to make my dream come true within the next two years. There is an old saying that if you want something badly enough and it is right that you should have it, then nothing will stop it happening. I want that horse to win at Ascot and I want it very badly. I have established that that horse has the blood in it to be a winner and despite what she has been through, the false registration, the dangers of being at the front in Flanders, her destiny having apparently been to draw a cart for the rest of her days – I just know that with the team I have gathered about her, she will win!"

Andrew could not help being infected with the Colonel's enthusiasm but the enormity of the task to which he had committed himself began to worry him. His mind was once more in a whirl but through the confusion one thought kept dominating – Colonel Marsh had said that Marion was one of the team he had selected to pursue his ambition with Jeannie. Peter had casually told him that he would be seeing more of Marion but he had thought of this as being in an office sense and yet, apparently by pure chance, Marion had been attending to Jeannie in her distress before he arrived from Scotland. Frankly, the idea that he might be working closely with her –

the woman he had begun to think of as 'the mystery woman' – thrilled him in a way that worried him. In the couple of busy days since he arrived the memory of that first hour in the stable had become a bit blurred but the very mention of the possibility of working closely with her disturbed him in a strange way.

These thoughts were flashing through his mind as they talked about Jeannie's future and started to sketch out a campaign plan for the months immediately ahead. Colonel Marsh was a man of decision; now that Andrew had decided that he was taking the job there were no hesitations – it was total commitment. They talked of the division of Andrew's time, reminding him that he had a heavy responsibility to carry for the rest of the stable enterprise. He had a lot to learn about the many facets of running an estate and business; he had the advantages of a good farming background, a lot of experience in handling people in his army days and some administrative experience gained after he was wounded but much would be new to him and he would have to learn and learn fast. Again, into his thoughts came the notion that Marion would help him even if he tried, rather feebly and without conviction, to banish such thoughts.

The forenoon passed with Colonel Marsh and Andrew discussing, planning, thinking and re-thinking how best to manage the estate and Jeannie. In the early afternoon Peter joined them for more talks. They agreed that Jeannie was now very much on the mend and thriving, much to the astonishment of the vets. Andrew said that he used her whenever possible to get around the estate on his business but had his eye on Hugh, one of the stable lads, to be a groom for Jeannie and to take her under his wing and start seriously working her. Andrew mentioned that Marion had started to ride Jeannie whenever she had a spare moment but he never mentioned that he had noticed that Jeannie showed the same affection for Marion as for him. Did the horse share the secret they both had buried deep in their hearts and minds? They finished the day in the office when Marion joined them for the first 'full team' conference to finalise their day's thoughts, with Marion preparing to put the results of their thinking on paper. Then Colonel Marsh announced that he would be away for the next few days and would leave things to them. Andrew was instructed to take steps to get his house ready and to arrange for his family to come down as soon as convenient.

AFTER A quiet supper in the kitchen with Peter and his family and, after he had paid a visit to Jeannie, Andrew retired to his room to write home and tell them all about the house and how he was going to get a number of jobs done to it before he sent for them in a few weeks. When he finally got to bed he fell asleep with his mind revolving round the new house, the prospect of Kirsty and the boys coming, the work he had to master on the estate, the training of Jeannie and how he would cope with the mysterious Marion. He dreamily realised that she was rather too often to the fore in his thoughts and this caused him a little concern, particularly since he found the thought of her rather pleasant. But he told himself very firmly that he had plenty to do in the ensuing months and maybe years without any involvement with another woman, however interesting and perhaps attractive she was. He was determined to keep his dealings with Marion on a strictly business basis, working with her as a member of the team but avoiding any entanglement. As he drifted to sleep, however, his last thoughts were, "Aye – she's some quine yon …!"

Chapter 5
The delights of London

Colonel Marsh was away for the best part of a week and 'the Jeannie team', as they had begun to call themselves, had made a great deal of progress. Jeannie was coming along nicely, back to her correct weight and literally 'eating like a horse'. Andrew had started to allow the stable lads to begin to stretch her, both on the flat and over the jumps. Indeed, on one of the first occasions when Andrew exerted his new authority he nominated Hugh, the youngest of the stable lads to be Jeannie's 'personal groom'. He had noticed that Jeannie was always happy when Hugh was tending or riding her and that he was popular with the other lads, so less likely to give rise to bad feelings or jealousy. Peter was helpful and very willing to pass on the knowledge he had gained over many years to this newcomer who was in some ways his 'boss'. Andrew for his part was particularly careful never to give any impression of 'throwing his weight about' and he and Peter very soon developed a very friendly working relationship. Both were in many ways lonely, Andrew being far from home and without his wife and family and Peter being rather devoid of male company at a social level where he could communicate.

The two men had long talks about many things and occasionally Andrew moved the conversation towards the subject of Marion but when Peter became strangely but politely silent and gently moved the chat on to another subject, Andrew was puzzled. It began to seem to him that everything about this woman was mysterious. He had known her for several weeks and had worked with her, she was a member of the family he lived with, he had been intimate with her in a most surprising manner and yet he knew very little about her. She fascinated him in a strange way, although he tried hard to keep their relationship on a purely business level – yet the memory of that first meeting was now, with the passage of time, taking on a decidedly rosy glow.

Andrew was now making arrangements to bring his family down from Scotland and work on the house was progressing well. He thought that all work would be finished by the end of another month and he asked the Colonel for permission to have a few days in Scotland with his family; a request, which was readily granted.

When he started to look up the Bradshaws in the office to find the best trains north, Marion suggested that he might be best to book a sleeper from London King's Cross to Aberdeen because it was a better journey to London than to Peterborough and easier to board at the terminal than have to wait at an intermediate station. Bookings were made so that Andrew would have time to buy a few gifts in London for Kirsty and the bairns before catching the sleeper. Then Marion suggested that, as she had some business to attend to in town, it would be sensible for Andrew to catch an earlier train and accompany her to London before Andrew's train left for Scotland. Andrew thought that this was a good idea because his wartime visits to London had always been hurried and he had seen very little of the capital. Peter drove them to Cambridge for the early train and they were in London by mid-afternoon, leaving them time for the shopping to be done before they enjoyed a leisurely lunch at a little restaurant, which Marion knew of in Soho.

In the afternoon they managed to see Buckingham Palace, Marble Arch, The Mall, Trafalgar Square and the Houses of Parliament, walking and using cabs to pack as much as possible into the short afternoon. To see so much would have been impossible but for Marion's knowledge of the city and the day ended, at Andrew's special request, with visits to the Cenotaph which had been erected a few years previously to the memory of the war dead and to the Tomb of the Unknown Warrior in Westminster Abbey. There were poignant moments for Andrew as his mind went back the dozen or so years to the different and more terrible world he had endured and to the colleagues he had left in France.

By the end of the afternoon they were both exhausted and Marion suggested that they should go to her hotel so that she could book in and they could have tea. This was a surprise to Andrew because he had thought that she was catching the early evening train back to Cambridge, his sleeper leaving at nine thirty. But it seemed a sensible suggestion and soon they were having a much-needed drink at the cocktail bar of the Sunburgh Hotel in Kensington, a modest but pleasant place in which Andrew felt quite at ease. The whole day had been an extreme pleasure to Andrew, to be escorted round London by such a knowledgeable and charming guide. It had been a revelation too, that Marion not only knew London so well but that she was so well-known in the various shops, restaurants and hotels that they had frequented. The surprises, however, were not over for the day. After a few drinks, Marion said she was in need of a freshen-up and suggested they use her room.

For the first time that day, Andrew felt distinctly ill at ease as they passed through the foyer to the stairs, past the reception where Marion collected her key. Poor Andrew was convinced that every eye was on him and that the hall porters and the call-boys with their extraordinary pill-box hats were nodding towards him, nudging one another and exchanging sly winks. It was all in his imagination of course, it was a matter of total indifference to them or only of interest if there was 'something' for them for their discretion. But it was not Andrew's imagination that unlocked Marion's door and entered her room. He knew it was very real and he had quite willingly (and it must be said happily) landed himself in this exciting and potentially dangerous situation. All day he had been close to her, in the train, in the restaurants and tearooms they had visited, in the cabs and in those moments of tremendous emotion as they stood at the Cenotaph and at the Unknown Soldier's Tomb, emotions he imagined Marion felt almost as strongly as he did.

As he shut the door and closed out the rest of the world, he turned to see her standing by the bed where she had laid her coat, looking at him intensely with eyes which said simply, "Please take me – and quickly." Andrew moved towards her, they were in each other's arms, their lips met hungrily and the bed welcomed them. There were but a few minutes of intense passion, with barely a moment wasted in removing garments, and it was over. Then, after some time in each other's embrace, Marion murmured, "Thank you, Andrew, I needed that," and they gently parted.

THEY BATHED together and before they dressed they lay on the sheets and made love again, this time slowly and gently until they were both fulfilled and content. When they rose to dress to go down for dinner, their mood was light and Andrew was smiling, "That was certainly more comfortable than the stable floor but I'll never forget that night."

"Nor will I," whispered Marion and the pair of them clung

to one another again like two young lovers, which they were, if not so young!

They ate together in a quiet corner of the dining room, with eyes hungry for one another and unashamedly enjoying their meal together. As time caught up with them and the time for Andrew to go approached, he decided to risk spoiling the atmosphere by saying, "Marion my dear – you remember why we are here. I am going back to Scotland to arrange to bring Kirsty and the bairns down here."

Marion said gently, "Andrew, I have lived long enough to be able to take what I want when I can enjoy it but I never want to cause any pain to anyone. No-one need be hurt by what we have done. And I have to really like someone when I want it. And I like you and God willing I might have you again without hurting anyone… but it will only be if there is pain for anyone."

Andrew said nothing, there was no need to – it had all been said. He kissed her lightly, gathered his gear and went out to start his long, lonely journey to Scotland and his wife and family.

Chapter 6
Andrew returns north

Back home at Blairmoss, he had that same odd feeling he used to experience when he was home on leave from France during the war, a strange feeling of not really belonging. Back from the horrors of the front he – along with many other soldiers who had experienced the awfulness of killing and living in dreadful conditions – developed a resentment against those who stayed at home. It was an involuntary reaction; they didn't deliberately generate this resentment. Often it was directed at their own loved ones and sometimes at those who, for real or contrived reasons, were of the age to fight but were still safely at home. It was as if there were an invisible curtain making it impossible to connect the veterans and those who were able to live ordinary, decent lives.

Now it was almost as if Andrew found himself on the other side of this curtain. After a mere month of living in the south, he saw the life he had left as something he wanted to be certain he had left for ever. He had subtly changed. It was not the people, his wife and family, his former boss, Blairmoss, the customers with whom he used to enjoy a chat and a laugh, the lads in the pub – no – perhaps it was just their way of life, their attitude to life, the crudeness, indeed coarseness, of life in the far north. Try as he would to break through the barrier, he couldn't! No, instead of – as in the war – the barrier keeping him away from the normality of their lives, it was preventing him from reverting to their normality.

Yet in many ways it was great to be home and Andrew let none of his feelings show. He asked himself a dozen times whether the feelings of which he was aware had anything to do with Marion but he was certain that the cause did not lie there. With Kirsty and the boys everything was as before. They talked excitedly about the impending move and he was plied with questions about the house, the school, who would their pals be? He described the stables and the horses. Their new house sounded grand compared with their cottar house at Blairmoss and there was a general air of anticipation in the family for the new life that lay ahead. He told them modestly about how he was now 'ane o' the mannies' on the estate, one of the bosses. He told them about the Colonel, about Peter and his family, about Jeannie and her new groom and about Marion, the Colonel's secretary, who played an important part in running the business. A date for the move was set at the end of the month. As far as the boys were concerned they would have gone back with him, the move couldn't have come soon enough. Kirsty, though, wanted a bit longer to get ready and, for one reason or another, she wanted to delay the uprooting process for another month, when the weather was warmer and at the end of the school term for the sake of the boy's education. Andrew agreed with Blairmoss on the end of his lease and the date was for three weeks' ahead. The long weekend was far too short and after fixing the railway people to flit them with a container, Andrew headed south once more, happy with the prospect of a permanent reunion with his family. He was less happy with the 'would not go away' feeling that he was glad to be leaving the austere life of the north and it had to be admitted – try as he would to deny it to himself – a happiness at the prospect of getting back to his new life in the softer countryside of Suffolk.

AT THE first team meeting on his return, Colonel Marsh reminded them that there was less than a year to go before their first attempt at Ascot and that Jeannie had a long way to go with her training. Her general fitness was now excellent and her stamina was building up to the extent that she could run the length of the Ascot course with a few jumps and not be hard stressed. They now had to plan next season's steeplechase programme so that she could build up racing experience without attracting too much attention from the racing world too soon. This would spoil her chances at Ascot. Meantime, the summer was to be hard work for her and for the team, carefully stretching her to her limit. They also had to think hard about a suitable racing name for her and they settled on Jeanokie, an easily remembered name, which had significance for those who knew her background. It rolled off the tongue and had a slightly continental ring about it. So Jeannie entered the world of competitive racing registered as Jeanokie. She was untried and unknown but with the blood of champions surging through her veins. A number of people – the sort who discreetly watched all the moves in the racing world, and noted all the registrations and studied the pedigrees – had already noticed her and had made casual visits to the area, chatting to the stable lads in the pubs, learning of Jeanokie's progress. What information they gleaned they kept to themselves; it was also in their interest that Jeanokie should not attract too much attention too soon.

When Andrew walked in to the office on his first day back, Marion was at her desk and she looked up and greeted him quite casually, asked how his journey had been and how his family was, all quite casual and conventional. Andrew had experienced butterflies when he entered the office; the picture in his mind was not the trim office madam but the pleasant creature he had left at the hotel dining table. Her ability to present a detached, cool, business-like but friendly aspect amazed him – she seemed to be almost two people in one. It was at times like this that Andrew felt very much the rude rustic, the unsophisticated countryman, perhaps outwardly calm but baffled as to how this woman – whom he had enjoyed and who had apparently been happy to be at one with him – was able to conceal her feelings, whatever they were, whenever she wished.

And so it continued in the weeks until the time approached for Kirsty and the boys to come down. Andrew had arranged to go up for them but a telegram arrived to say that Kirsty was down with influenza and was unable to travel. He phoned Blairmoss in the evening and he indicated that Kirsty, although unwell, was not ill enough to justify Andrew coming up. Deeply disappointed, Andrew decided that since all the work on the house was completed, he would not impose himself on Peter and his family any longer but would move into his house and 'bothy it' until Kirsty was able to come down. In their letters, Andrew and Kirsty agreed on some of the curtains and some other domestic details and with the help of a lady from the village who acted as Mrs Marsh's seamstress, he got the house curtained. The floor coverings were already down and Andrew took it upon himself to order some living room and bedroom furniture, some kitchen stuff and so on to make life more comfortable.

Weeks went by but the letter from Kirsty saying she was fit and ready did not arrive and Andrew made up his mind to go up north to assess the situation at first hand. Meantime he was quite comfortable in his house by himself, with enough goods in the house to meet his simple needs. Cooking for himself was no problem, his experience as a young farmhand and as a soldier served him well. Any monotony of his own cooking was relieved by the regular twice-weekly invitations he had to eat at Peter's house as well as the occasional invitation to spend an evening with some of the other families on the estate.

As for Marion, there was never an invitation to her place in the clock tower above the stable and he never plucked up courage to have her over to his house, even on a daytime visit. He had tacitly assumed that such an invitation would wait until his family were settled in, although Marion had been much involved in the preparing of the house, ordering tradesmen and buying things. It was not that the thought of a visit by her didn't occur to Andrew, often in the evenings and sometimes during his lonely nights.

Eventually Andrew made the journey north again and before he came away he had a promise from Kirsty to be down on the first day after the school broke up for the long summer break in ten days' time. This time he made all the arrangements with Blairmoss, the railway company and some of his friends so that Kirsty and the boys would manage to travel on their own; he would meet them at Peterborough. As he travelled south he felt an unease, a feeling that despite his efforts things might not work out as he intended. Despite that, on a glorious summer evening, heavy with heat as evenings can be in that flat area, Kirsty and two very excited boys got off the express at Peterborough. Almost before he had time to say hello, Andrew was dragged down the platform to see the *Gresley Pacific* steam locomotive, which had brought them down from Edinburgh at, "near a hunner miles an 'oor, Dad!" He had probably told the lads about these huge locomotives, the like of which they had never seen on the railways north of Aberdeen, so it was a great thrill to be lifted briefly up onto the footplate to see the roaring fire through the firebox door, before they were handed unceremoniously back to their father as whistles blew, the monster hissed and thundered off toward London King's Cross.

Andrew had been given the use of Peter's estate truck and it was a memorable evening for them all as they drove, crowded into the tiny cab – with their luggage tied on to the platform behind – into the gloaming, towards Cambridge, the estate and the house that was to be their new home.

Chapter 7
A stranger in the stables

Visiting the stables one day soon after Kirsty and the boys had arrived, Andrew was a bit surprised when Peter asked him, more formally than usual, if he could have a word. Sensing that something was worrying Peter, Andrew suggested that they have a couple of horses saddled so that they could have a ride around the estate and talk uninterrupted and unobserved. When Andrew asked what was bothering him, Peter hesitated before admitting that he was not certain if his worry was real or imagined but he went on to tell how he had taken on this stable lad who had turned out to be good at his job and Peter's worry was that he was just too good. At his interview he had claimed some experience of handling horses but Peter had observed, and it had been remarked on by others, that this man was highly skilled. In addition, Peter had noted that he was obsequious to the point of irritation in his dealings with Peter and the other, long-established lads. At first he had put this down to his newness but after a bit Peter decided that his ingratiating manner was not genuine and he wondered why. A chance remark by one of his jockeys that the new man seemed to have a special interest in Jeanokie and had been casually asking a lot of questions about how she was performing made Peter feel ill at ease.

The two men agreed that this man was worth watching and a plan of action was worked out. Some of the stable lads whom they could trust implicitly were to be taken into their confidence and Jeanokie's steadily improving performance was to be 'camouflaged' by the lads by simply holding her back when there were others, especially the inquisitive one, around and that false times and other figures were to be fed to him. They decided against sacking him straight away because he might, given time, say or do something to give them a clue as to who was especially interested in the horse.

Meantime Andrew was getting his family settled in. The boys were over the moon with everything, the house, the freedom they had and the friends they quickly made. Of course they were all on holiday and the long summer days were spent exploring the estate and finding out what they were allowed to do and what they could not. Certain areas were completely out of bounds, close to the 'big house', for example, and where there was danger from galloping horses. Despite these restrictions there were plenty of things to see, do and learn. The estate had its own sawmill and before long they were allowed to lead the gentle but powerful shire horses, which hauled the huge logs from the woods to the mill. The blacksmith's shop intrigued them and they never tired of watching the racehorses having their shoes changed in accordance with their training needs. So the long summer days passed pleasantly for them and in the evenings they had their dad with them to answer, or attempt to answer, their endless questions.

With Kirsty, however, things were different. When she arrived at their new home after that journey in the truck from Peterborough, with the boys bubbling with excitement from both the train journey and anticipation, Kirsty was moody. Her scarcely concealed lack of enthusiasm for the house, its décor and its furnishings, as far as they went, was a great disappointment to Andrew who, having been forced to act on his own, had tried to make his choices with what he thought she would like in mind. At first he put it down to tiredness, or a reaction to being pulled away from her roots and dread that she wouldn't be able to match up to Andrew's new style of life. Though, as the days went on Andrew became seriously worried; Kirsty never complained about anything but Andrew could not get over her complete lack of enthusiasm, her apathy and unwillingness to try anything new. Being country-bred, she was a competent rider but – even with a whole range of horses at her disposal and Andrew's offer to kit her out with the riding habit worn by the ladies of the area – she very seldom rode.

She established a working, rather than a friendly, relationship with Peter's wife, Joan, who had tried to do everything possible to make her welcome into their society. Andrew realised that – with him out all day at work and with the boys hardly ever in, as there was so much for them to do – she was lonely and feeling far from home. He had of course hoped that the thrill of the new, quite grand house would have stimulated her and that she would have wanted to put her stamp on it. Joan and the other ladies had taken her to the Women's Royal Institute (WRI), the Guild and other organisations, which were still operating through the summer and while she went along, it was without enthusiasm. Did she feel out of place with her rather broad Scottish accent? Everybody assured her that they loved to hear her speak and found no difficulty in understanding her – indeed she was understood more easily than she herself understood many of the locals with their Suffolk tongues.

Strangely enough, when she first met Marion, a bond was

quickly established between them and they became friends, with Marion soon becoming Kirsty's confidant. When Andrew first realised that this was happening, he was apprehensive. Then he remembered Marion's capacity for neither talking nor even showing her feelings when she didn't want to, and he was glad in a way that Kirsty had found a friend. He welcomed anything that would help to get her settled but this was mixed with the vague fear of what would happen if there were to be any development of his relationship with Marion. In his quiet moments of reflection, he alternated between worrying about the fear of his past misdeeds being discovered, being confident in the knowledge that the only other person who know of these events was completely discreet and a vague longing for an opportunity for these misdeeds to be repeated. So, just as in the office where they were simply work colleagues, a relationship of firm family friends developed between Andrew and Marion. This arrangement suited all three parties; it certainly seemed to help Kirsty and she appeared to try to integrate into the small community.

As the summer wore on, the plot to find out more about the new stable lad who had caused concern had been put into operation and seemed to be successful. Those involved were convinced, by noting his apparently harmless casual questions that he was a 'plant' and had been inveigled into the stable to spy on the performance of Jeanokie. The question was by whom? The team decided that they had enough to involve Colonel Marsh and when he heard the story he was pleased with what had been done but worried about the seriousness of the whole affair. His main concern was to find out who was behind it and he undertook to discreetly follow this up himself through his own contacts.

The team was instructed to devise a scheme whereby the intruder could be removed from the scene without his suspicions being roused, on some excuse unrelated to his job or to horses. This seemed as if it would be difficult because the man made it his business never to step out of line, either at work or in his dealings with the other lads but it was Ray, one of the 'trustees' amongst the stable lads who solved the problem. Amongst the many skills which Mick, the man under suspicion, possessed was considerable skill at throwing darts and he was a leading member, if not the star, of the local pub team, the Black Bullsters. The Bullsters had reached the finals of the Cambridge Cup and the final was due to take place in a pub called The Oatbridge the following Saturday.

Now Ray had a pal, an electrician, who frequently did jobs in The Oatbridge and he had been asked to improve the lighting for the darts final and install spotlights on the board and the scoreboard. The idea was devised whereby Ray's pal would install – concealed behind the panelling, which carried the dart board – a small but powerful electromagnet which could be energised by a switch, which in turn was operated by closing a small cupboard door at the other side of the public bar. The idea was that when Mick threw a vital dart, the magnet would be switched on and its pull would be sufficient to deflect the flight of the steel tip of the dart enough to convert a good 'twenty' to a miserable 'one' or a 'sixty' to a 'three'. It had been tested thoroughly in the jockey's room at the stable; it was in some ways a dirty trick but they justified it because they were convinced that they were involved in a dirty game. All of this was planned to get Mick so ruffled that, when he couldn't achieve his usual level of skill in front of an audience, he would drop his 'nice chap' image and do something to cause the game to be abandoned. If all went according to plan, and he was a fake and lost his temper, then the game would have to be replayed without him on a fair basis. His actions would give the landlord an excuse to put him out and an estate employee behaving badly in the local would be regarded as a reflection on the estate and give the estate an excuse to sack him.

And it worked all right on the big night. Mick at the dartboard was somewhat arrogant, he knew he was good and liked to make sure all eyes were on him when he had to throw a vital double. Every now and again his dart failed to score and he thought he was having a bad night. Then he was back on form until another important dart went wrong and he reached for another Guinness. Before the evening was half through he was on to the dark rums and from then on it was downhill; when a treble twenty went wrong he threw his next dart with such force in temper that it hit a wire and bounced back into the watchers. A young lad got the dart through the fleshy part of his little finger, fortunately missing the bone but causing him considerable distress. Mick, with the drink getting hold of him, shouted that he shouldn't have been standing so close – no concern, no apology, just anger that he had missed. A rather unpleasant scene developed and as a result Mick was carted off to spend the night in the care of Constable Connach.

Next day, on his release on bail from the various charges, Andrew sacked Mick and asked him to leave immediately but not before his locker was opened and the contents examined. Sure enough, a list of all Jeanokie's performances over the past two weeks was found along with a series of comments in Mick's handwriting, which showed him to be a man skilled in judging horseflesh. Most important of all was the name of Mick's correspondent, at a London address. When he was informed of these developments, Colonel Marsh was delighted but when he saw the name and address of the person who was being sent the information he paled visibly. Without explaining further, he asked Andrew and Peter to emphasise to all concerned the need for the utmost secrecy and discretion about what was going on. When he was alone with Andrew he said that the man in London was a man with whom he had had unpleasant dealings before the war and that there was a connection with Marion. For this reason, he didn't want the name mentioned to her.

Chapter 8
America bound

Kirsty found it difficult to adjust to life in the south. She had a very comfortable house, money was no great problem, the boys were settled down and enjoying themselves with their new-found friends and Andrew was busy at his work, engrossed in it even. Perhaps it was the fact that she was now forced to live the life of a lady and, housework apart, she had so little to do compared with the busy life she had led up until now. She found that she was living a lonely life and with Andrew away at work all day and often in the evenings, the boys out all day playing with their pals in their spare time, her only real friend was Marion but she too led a very busy life and they met only occasionally.

The lack of enthusiasm, which she showed for their new home when she first arrived did not really diminish with time. Andrew thought that perhaps it was because he had been responsible for getting it, decorating and furnishing it; she had very little input so he encouraged her to change things and even redecorate to her tastes. The response was usually an apathetic, "We'll nae bother – it's the wye ye winted it so it'll dae fine."

Even when she first came down there had still been furniture to choose but that had been done without enthusiasm. A degree of irritation started to develop between them, niggling followed by long silences and sometimes open quarrelling.

By the time the summer was past and the boys were back at school, Andrew decided to have a down-to-earth talk with her. He felt, not unreasonably, that he had done the best he could for her and the boys and that he needed domestic peace so that he could get on with his work, which he thought of as the provider of all. After some defiant posturing Kirsty suddenly burst into tears and cried, "Ach! Anra, I'm jist needin' hame. I canna thole it doon here an' I niver will. Gaun aboot wi naethin tae dee a day – its nae my wye o' daen' things."

Poor Andrew was at a complete loss as to what to say and he tried to point out that the boys were very happy here and would perhaps have a better chance in life than they would in the north. He said that with the winter coming on there would be lots of evening activities in the school, evening classes in sewing and needlework and sports such as badminton. There was also the Women's Institute, which she could join and that if she could learn to drive he would get her a small car so that she could get to these activities under her own steam. So she agreed to give it a little longer and to Andrew's relief things seemed to settle down when the next event, which would dramatically affect Andrew's life, happened.

HE HAD a message that Colonel Marsh would like to see him that evening at the Hall. Now Andrew had been there on several occasions but never of an evening and he wondered what it was all about. When the maid ushered him into the Colonel's study, he found him alone with a bottle of whisky and two glasses on the desk.

"Good of you to come, Andrew, at such short notice. I hope I didn't interrupt any plans you had."

"No! no! Colonel, the bowling season is finished now and my evenings are not so much taken up," replied Andrew.

"Well, I want you to undertake a very important, and in many ways a very delicate, task for me. I am very pleased with the way you all handled the business of the man who was planted on us to spy on Jeanokie and, in particular, the way you arranged to get rid of him without involving the stables and the horses. You remember that I told you that I would discreetly investigate the man behind the spying, and suggested that the name should be kept from Marion? I don't wish to say much more about the connection but sufficient to say I have made discreet enquiries through some of my contacts in town and I am sure we have to be very careful with Jeanokie. He is a bad man. Now I have decided to send Jeanokie to my cousin's ranch in Colorado, near a small town called Last Chance and I want you to go there to make the necessary arrangements and await Jeanokie's arrival. I am asking Marion to go with you, she has met my cousin and his family and there will be enough work for you both. Now I hope Mrs Sproat has settled down and will manage while you are away."

Andrew managed after a struggle to say, "Yes," his mind in a complete whirl. He had talked Kirsty into settling down again and now he would have to tell her that he was leaving her completely on her own for at least a couple of months, for that was the time they thought it would take to make the arrangements and get the horse over to America and settled in. However, the thing that made his stomach turn over was the thought that Marion was going with him. Now he had no worries on the score of Kirsty suspecting anything; Marion and he had been very circumspect about the two events, the night of his arrival and in London and he had begun to think that it might all be over, thankfully. Now, he both feared and looked forward to the new and intriguing situation, which had been landed on them.

Kirsty took it well, too quietly perhaps, when Andrew explained that it was simply part of his job and he was probably the only person who could do it. Nothing was said about Marion going too, that seemed to be accepted and preparations were well ahead for the trip when something happened, which caused them all to worry and fear. Kilwinnock, a mare with remarkably similar markings to Jeanokie and who was stabled next to her, was found dead one morning. She had been perfectly fit the evening before, galloping hard with the rest on her evening workout. Next day the vets reported back with the result of their post mortem – Kilwinnock had undoubtedly died of poisoning, probably administered in a sweet like a Mars Bar fed as a treat after the normal evening feed.

Colonel Marsh had no option but to call in the police and investigate the matter openly. He was inclined at first to employ a detective agency who could be discreet but his insurance company wanted the police brought in and they questioned the entire stable staff, starting at the top. They were told of course about the 'plant', they already knew of the reason for his sudden departure from the area and Colonel Marsh told them as much as he could about the people in London whom he suspected were involved in some way with the dubious stable lad. He had of course to be very careful about this information, partly because it had been given to him in confidence and also because of the mysterious involvement with Marion. Quite early in the investigation, the local Inspector had called for assistance from the CID in Cambridge and Detective Inspector Baxter took charge.

He soon became very interested in the story of Jeanokie, the special interest that both Colonel Marsh and the shadowy people in London had in the horse's performance, the man who had obviously been planted there and the fact that someone had poisoned not Jeanokie but a similar horse in the adjoining stable. He instigated a deeper inquiry into the activities of the several betting rings known to operate and in turn enlisted the help of a contact he had in the Metropolitan Police.

The death of Kilwinnock cast a gloom over the stable, a gloom mixed with an uncomfortable foreboding, a feeling that worse was to come. Rumour soon had it that the poisoning had been intended for Jeanokie and not Killwinnock and that it had been done as a spiteful act by the fake stable boy, spiteful or as a revenge on the rest of the stable crew who had engineered his removal. The considerable level of police activity fuelled the rumours and it was soon being circulated that a racing syndicate based in London wanted to get their hands on the stable; they were intending to dishearten Colonel Marsh by getting rid of his best horses. Amongst the stories and rumours, bits and pieces of the story of Jeannie that was now Jeanokie began to become known, how she had been discovered by Colonel Marsh and there were whispers of his hopes for her in the big-time racing world. Such gossip being widely circulated was the last thing the Colonel wanted and he resolved to speed up his plans to get Jeanokie away to America into anonymity and safety.

There was frantic activity arranging the journey, export and import licences, veterinary certificates and various other documents for the horse and passports and visas for Marion and Andrew, as well as currency arrangements. Marion and the Colonel handled most of these things and eventually Marion and Andrew were booked on 25th September, 1932 on the *RMS Mauretania* out of Southampton to New York and Jeanokie would travel by cargo boat from Liverpool to Chicago in the charge of Hugh, the stable lad whom Andrew had selected as her personal groom and who had turned out to be everything Andrew had expected of him. Jeanokie would be safe in his charge and the longer sea journey would result in a shorter rail trip from Chicago and then by road to Faith. They had two weeks to go before they sailed and there was a great deal to do. Andrew spent much time poring over a map of America, finding out where this place was with the intriguing but slightly ominous name of Last Chance. He found that its nearest railhead was Denver and that Denver lay on the Union Pacific Platte Valley Transcontinental line. He thought his best plan would be to head for Last Chance from New York by rail via Indianapolis, St Louis, Kansas City and on to Denver, from where they would be picked up by their hosts. Then, after they were settled, he would travel by Union Pacific to Chicago by way of Omaha to meet Jeanokie and Hugh off the boat and escort them to their new temporary home on the ranch.

As he studied the maps and familiarised himself with the names of those faraway places, Andrew could hardly believe how a kindly fate had dealt with him; how, within a year he, a milk roundsman from the far north of Scotland was getting the opportunity to travel to the mighty United States of America, almost traverse the continent and visit places with such romantic names as St Louis. On top of that, however much he tried to banish it from is mind, the thought that he was to make this journey in the stimulating company of Marion was a pleasing one. He found time to acquire a pony and trap for Kirsty to use while he was away, to help them get around. He had hoped that she would have learned to drive but there wasn't enough time.

The departure from the Colonel's estate was a strange mixture of excitement, worry and trepidation, even fear. Andrew hated leaving Kirsty and the boys, especially since they had been a relatively short time in England; he was less worried about the lads than about Kirsty – the boys had friends and were happy but Kirsty was strange and distant. Andrew worried because she would be not only without him but without Marion on whom she had come to rely for advice and companionship, rather more perhaps than Andrew liked. He had felt for some time that instead of learning to be herself she was content to let Marion guide her in the most trivial things. He had done everything in the limited time available to ensure that she would cope in his absence and Peter and the Colonel had assured him that they and their wives would look after her. Andrew still had a strange sense of uneasiness as he kissed Kirsty goodbye and the faraway look in her eyes stayed with him as the train took them to London and Southampton, on their way to far-away America.

Chapter 9
Across the Atlantic

Jeanokie was to be secretly taken by lorry horse box from the estate and put in a rail horse box destined for Liverpool. After her wartime experiences she was quite used to travelling and as long as she had someone she trusted to hand she seemed to almost enjoy the hustle-bustle of travelling. Because of the suspicion that she was the real object of the poison attack, the police had told the authorities the route she was to take and a discreet watch was kept on the horse box as it made its way towards Liverpool. The marshalling yards were the biggest cause of concern, particularly when the box was in a remote siding and on these occasions Hugh slept in the box with her. She was due to arrive in America ten days after Andrew and Marion and it had been arranged that Andrew would meet the boat at Milwaukie as soon as she berthed. It seemed that everything possible had been done to ensure the safety of the horse so Andrew and Marion felt they could relax and enjoy the trip across the Atlantic on the *RMS Mauretania*.

And enjoy the trip they did. They were travelling second

class and this gave them a considerable level of luxury, with comfortable berths and a very high standard of dining facilities and travelling as they were in late autumn, or in the 'fall' in the transatlantic way of speaking, the weather was fine, with calm seas and little wind. Much of the day could be spent on deck, either enjoying the varied activities organised by the crew: quoits, deck tennis and suchlike or pampering themselves lounging on deck chairs and being waited on hand and foot. They soon made friends with some of their fellow passengers and this increased the enjoyment of the trip, especially in the evenings when they gathered in one of the very pleasant cocktail bars for a drink before going in to eat. Eating was, of course, one of the highlights of the trip, with each meal seemingly an attempt to outdo the previous one for quality and quantity. Andrew had never been fed so well in his whole life and after a few days he began to worry about his figure – after all he was at the stage when 'middle age spread' was a distinct possibility. Even Marion, who was one of the types who could eat well and never show it, began to ease off after a few days. Often parts of the afternoons and evenings were spent in the lounges playing cards with their new-found friends or playing 'housie-housie'. One of the enjoyable events, which enlivened the day was the daily sweepstake on how far the ship had travelled the previous day as measured by the ship's log, the distance being declared under the hand of the captain and posted around the ship's notice boards at eleven o'clock exactly.

So the days at sea passed extremely pleasantly, eating, sleeping, having a modest drink, lounging on deck, playing games or having a small gamble either on the daily log or in the casinos. Andrew and Marion were spending most of their waking hours together and were quite frankly enjoying one another's company. For the first few days at sea they had been quite circumspect, as if by mutual consent. They said goodnight to one another after the pleasant evenings together and went their separate ways but on the third night out, the word went round the passengers that phosphorescence could be seen in the ship's wake after dark. This phenomenon is caused by microscopic organisms in the water being activated and caused to give out light in the maelstrom caused by the propeller and the wake from the ship thrashing through the water. This phosphorescence is a magnificent sight when viewed from the stern of the ship, a long line of glowing white, widening into the distance, a ghostly sight that, once seen, can never be forgotten.

It was a glorious September evening as the passengers stood and watched the phenomenon, the ladies warmed by their furs or wraps against the slight chill, which was felt as the night wore on. In pairs and groups, the passengers drifted off to the bars or their beds and Andrew and Marion found themselves alone, leaning on the stern rail, enchanted with the sight, the pleasantness of the evening and themselves. With a slight shiver as a wisp of wind chilled her, Marion moved closer to Andrew and he put a protective arm around her as she snuggled to him. Suddenly the emotion, which had bonded them since that first encounter but which had been mutually suppressed except for the lapse in London, now overpowered them and they were in each other's arms, locked in embrace as if to death and longing for fulfilment. They walked, still clinging to one another, to their cabins but needed only one key.

They awoke in the early morning when Andrew nearly fell out of the bunk, which had been adequate for them when awake but not wide enough to combat the gentle roll of the ship. To avoid the mild (if any) embarrassment to the cabin maid when she brought the morning tea, they decided to dress and find a secluded corner where they could have a coffee and a talk. They both felt a suggestion of tension between them, something which had never been there before and they felt the need to talk about their situation, a thing they had seldom done. As they walked through the sleeping ship to an upper deck, still full of tenderness for one another, Andrew realised the problem that would face them over the next few weeks. However strong his resolution had been, he knew now that he could not fight it and he was fairly certain that it was the same with Marion. He remembered her determined viewpoint that she would accept it only if nobody got hurt but he was anxious to know if she still felt like that. He was conscious that he knew so little about Marion, despite having worked with her for many months and always at the back of his mind were the few snippets that he did know, from Colonel Marsh's revelation that there was a connection between Marion and the 'man in London' – who was somehow on the fringes of the police investigation of the poisoning – and the odd way in which their mutual friend Peter had declined to ever talk about her. He recalled that he had been told that her husband had been the Colonel's Adjutant and that he had been killed just as the war was close to ending.

The two middle-aged lovers, for such they were, found a corner of the morning lounge on C deck, cleaned and manned ready for the early risers, the keep-fit addicts in need of refreshment after their early morning run round the deck and the hard drinkers in need of coffee to purge their systems. They drank their coffee, looked and smiled at each other before Marion broke the silence.

"We need to talk and say much to one another," she said.

"Andrew, I need you, want you and love you but I am not going to steal you. Even if you come to me of your own volition I will not accept you permanently because Kirsty and the boys would suffer, must suffer and ultimately you would suffer."

Andrew poured another cup of coffee for them, drank slowly to give himself time to think, realising that deep philosophical discussions such as they were embarking upon were not his forte and knowing at the same time that such talk was essential. Then out of the blue he found himself asking for the answer to what had been puzzling and worrying him since almost their first meeting. The way he phrased the question now is how he would have earlier, had he thought it out. He felt that there could be no rationale until he knew the answer to the question he bluntly asked, "Marion, who are you and why are you here?"

As he said it he realised what a blunt, brutal question it was, one to which most people would react with anger, or be defensive, or simply remain silent, or get up and leave.

Marion did none of these things. She sat quietly for several minutes, obviously thinking deeply, her eyes filling with tears. Marion had never before allowed herself to show emotion; she had hitherto presented an implacable face, always pleasant, always polite, always ready to listen but seldom, even never, showing her inner feelings. It was almost as if she wore a mask, which she never let slip. It was a facility that enabled her to face most situations in life without revealing her thoughts and was the envy of many people whose face told all. Except here – sitting in a corner of a ship-board coffee house, early in the morning after a highly emotional night with the man she now had to admit to herself she loved – the mask slipped.

"Not now Andrew," she said in a whisper. "Tonight we will have dinner in the White Star Room and after that I will tell you what you deserve to know," and with that Andrew had to be content for the time being.

Chapter 10
Marion tells all

The rest of that day passed in the usual pleasant way. After a swim in the tiny pool, they enjoyed a leisurely Turkish bath followed by a light lunch and then a siesta until it was cinema time when they watched a Buster Keaton comedy. There was no tension between them but a feeling of anticipation of an evening, which promised to be memorable. The White Star Room was perhaps the crown of all the dining rooms on the *Mauretania*, open to all classes aboard ship (provided they could afford it) and was used for special occasions, by people celebrating anniversaries and suchlike, for wining and dining friends and business colleagues and for tête-à-têtes like the one Andrew and Marion were intending. It was a superb room with opulent furnishings and pleasantly subdued lighting. Each table, magnificently set with places for two, four or many people was so placed that it was out of earshot of the neighbouring one, the peripheral tables being set in alcoves. Palm and other plants were strategically placed to provide additional screening and a seven-piece orchestra played unobtrusively in its recess in the middle of one long wall. The staff, dressed either in immaculate evening dress or uniform, hovered around the diners rather like ghosts, present but unseen until their services were required. They acted under the control of a number of senior waiters, who each had responsibility for a small group of tables. A diner had but to raise a finger, or give some other indication, for a waiter to be at his or her side, enquiring how he could be of service.

Into this room, at eight o'clock precisely, entered Marion and Andrew. Marion in an elegant blue dress enhanced by a simple gold necklace and bracelet and highlighted by a diamond cluster at her cleavage and Andrew resplendent in Highland evening dress. Andrew had got his evening dress together in the weeks before he left for America, some of the accessories were borrowed but he had brought his kilt in his favourite tartan, Ancient Stewart of Appin. Even in such elegant company as occupied the White Star Room, eyes turned as they walked in and Andrew was glad when they were seated at their table. Never before had he been in such a 'posh' place and although in his recent life he was gradually becoming inured to what might be called 'the high life', he was conscious of his humble background, relieved only by the knowledge that Marion was at his side.

The dinner itself beggared description. When they had decided to book into the White Star Room they had agreed that nothing would be spared, a 'hang the expense' attitude and they went through the incredible menu as if it was to be their last meal on earth. Each of the seven courses surpassed the previous one and for Andrew the highlight was a grouse dish, especially when the waiter assured him that the birds were flying over the moors of Scotland a few days before they sailed. With a full quota of the appropriate wine with every course – the ship's 'cellars' kept only the best – they were a very mellow couple when they reached the coffee and liqueur stage. By this time, it was well past midnight and the restaurant was emptying. At their suggestion they were left to themselves with a pot of coffee on a spirit burner, a bottle of Drambuie for Andrew and Crème de Menthe, which was Marion's choice.

During the meal there had been no serious conversation but now, when they were settled entirely by themselves in the corner, Marion said, "Now, Andrew, I will put your mind at rest and tell you about myself. Whether or not you will still feel the same about me when you know the whole story remains to be seen but it is only fair to you that I tell you and leave you to decide."

Andrew, relaxed but intrigued at what he might hear leaned back in his luxurious leather-backed dining chair and nodded as an invitation for her to continue.

"I am forty-six years old, an odd confession for a woman to be making but this is an occasion for telling the truth. I was born to what can be described as an upper-middle class family in Esher, a select village in the south-east suburbs of London. My father was a doctor who had spent his early life in India and married the daughter of an army brigadier. Our family was pretty typical of the late Victorian era and I was brought up in the rigid, respectable – looking back to my childhood – rather boring atmosphere of the time. Everything had to be so 'proper' and there was the inevitable nanny to see that everything was 'so' and later, at the 'correct' school I attended, conformation was dinned into us so that initiative became stifled. I found it so boring that I'm afraid I tried to rebel when I was sixteen and was temporarily expelled, sent home to face the wrath of my father and the disappointment of my mother. 'Rebellion' in those days was something not tolerated in our society and I could be allowed back to school only if I was sufficiently contrite. So I was 'sentenced' by my father to stay with an aunt in Guernsey in the Channel Isles until the start of the next academic year."

At this point in her story Marion smiled quietly to herself as she continued, "I've never been sure whether or not there was a sympathy lurking in the heart of my mother, which ensured that my 'sentence' was such a kind one. It might even have been my father who knew what he was doing by sending me to Guernsey, giving me a second chance while outwardly being very strict. At all events it was a wonderful 'sentence' because I simply loved life in St Peter Port where my aunt lived. She was headmistress of a school run by the Warden and Bailiffs of the island and I had the advantage of really having my own teacher while attending a pretty good school. The atmosphere in my aunt's home and at school was so different from my home and school, there was a degree of freedom, which I had never experienced before and I made the most of it. At the same time, I was quite academically inclined and worked hard at my lessons, I really wanted to progress and go to university to be a doctor if at all possible. I had heard such a lot about the struggles women had endured to become doctors and how the war had helped women to find their rightful place in society. My family agreed that I could stay in Guernsey for another year and in that time I got the qualifications that I needed to go to university."

Andrew had never heard Marion say so much at one time and was completely absorbed in the story she was telling him. He noticed, however, that at this point in her story her mood had changed to sombre as she continued.

"Much as I enjoyed life in Guernsey, it was then that my life started to go wrong. I was sixteen going seventeen, well developed both mentally and physically, still with a rebellious streak and desperate to get to grips with life. I loved and was very grateful to my aunt and wouldn't have done a thing to hurt or embarrass her but I met a young man called Alan at a party and Oh, Dear! I didn't know what hit me. I know now, of course, that he was a typical cad of the worse type but at that time, to me, he was a hero, a man-about-town, full of panache, plenty of charm, wealthy and I fell for him completely and absolutely. He moved in the same society circle as my aunt and my infatuation went apparently unnoticed. For all the time we associated in Guernsey nothing improper took place and to be honest it wasn't for me not wanting it to happen. Perhaps he was very cunning, I don't really know to this day but he kept things under control, perhaps because he couldn't risk anything happening, which would make him 'persona non grata' in our society. I should have said he was in his middle twenties, about eight years older than me. Remember that in those post-Victorian days it was not unusual for a girl to marry a man several years her senior, in fact it was normal for a man to have made progress in his career before he sought a lady's hand in marriage. But I confess I didn't have marriage in mind, I just wanted a good time and to have my own career, I still wanted to be a doctor."

There was a pause as she stretched out for her coffee cup and Andrew poured them both a fresh cup and at the same time charged their now empty glasses. A hovering waiter was waved away and with his eyes Andrew invited Marion to continue.

"At the end of my extra year in Guernsey I had gained admission to my father's old college in Oxford to study medicine and it was time to say farewell to my aunt, her family and to Alan. To be honest it was more difficult to part from my adoptive family than from Alan, I think I was growing up and at the same time growing tired of him. The picture he painted of himself was quite an intriguing one; he said he was the son of an army major who had been killed in action in Africa during the Zulu wars and that he lived on a settlement made on him by the senior naval officer with whom his widowed mother cohabited. He maintained that despite the generous settlement, he was estranged from his mother and never saw her or her consort and explained his lengthy absences from Guernsey by his need to attend to his property business in London. All of this nonsense we all accepted at the time, although I now know that he lived off his father who adored him and who had a prosperous pub in the East End of London. His father had paid generously to have him attend a 'School for Gentlemen' near Rugby, where he had acquired the trappings and style of a gentleman so that these, coupled with his native wit, equipped him for the easy life, based on the deceit and deception, which he had chosen."

Marion went on to tell how she had barely settled in to her new life in college in Oxford when Alan turned up quite unexpectedly. She had received him courteously but wished that he had not come back into her life and resolved to discourage him, something which proved very difficult because he very quickly ingratiated himself with her circle of friends in her college. They all thought he was wonderful, such a gallant fellow and before long he was part of the 'gang', even though he had no link with the university.

Marion explained, "I found myself in an impossible situation. Alan seemed to be always around and some of the old infatuation returned but now he started to put pressure on me to become his mistress and whereas a year or so ago I would happily have done so but for fear of letting my aunt down, now I was scared of spoiling my university career by becoming pregnant. I pleaded for time to decide what I was going to do and it was when he was away on one of his 'business trips' that I began to learn things about him. My friends were telling me how lucky I was to have such a hero for a boyfriend, it appeared he had been telling them how, when he was touring the world as a mercenary, he had been in one of the South American countries during one of their revolutions and he had saved the life of the President by hauling him out of the water when he fell overboard when jumping ashore to escape. The President was so grateful that he made Alan a Companion of

Honour when the revolution was squashed. He had also been regaling the impressionable young students with stories of how he had been caught gun-running and had been imprisoned in chains in a ghastly dungeon, to be freed eventually by the intervention of the British Ambassador who happened to be a friend of his mother's consort. None of this was true."

Marion went on to explain to Andrew how, like the other students, she had believed what Alan had said about himself and had been impressed but when, on his return, he became more demanding and when she still held him off, he several times hinted that he might tell her aunt that their relationship in Guernsey had not been entirely innocent. Marion knew this to be untrue and regarded the threat as a nasty form of blackmail. Even though she feared him and the damage he might do, she did not yield and rather to her surprise he put on the charm again and a relationship similar to that which they had in Guernsey developed, except that his absences 'on business' became longer and more frequent. This situation continued until the end of Marion's third year when he reappeared just in time for the end-of-term ball. Her third year was, as usual in the medical faculty, a particularly stressful and difficult one and Marion was tensed like a fiddle string. The results came out on the day of the ball, she had passed with flying colours, she was beside herself with relief, Alan was with her at the ball and afterwards, her defences came down.

By the beginning of what should have been her fourth year Marion knew that she could not continue her studies with a child inside her. Alan made no objections to their getting married, except that he wanted an elaborate conventional wedding whereas Marion was adamant that it had to be a registry office affair with no fuss. She wanted to move from Oxford but he found her a modest flat and left her there as he carried on with his comings and goings, often leaving her without much money. In her new position as wife, Marion tried, gently at first, to probe his background and was, often light-heartedly fobbed off. When she became a bit more persistent he would show anger and suggest that it was none of her business. Then as her time drew near, Marion became ill and it was confirmed that the birth was going to be difficult. At the very time when his presence was most needed, Alan disappeared and Marion had to seek help from her parents, who had hitherto been supportive without in any way interfering. Her father moved her to Esher so that he could help her at the birth but his dedicated efforts were to no avail and the baby died. Marion of course survived and quickly recovered. Her father decided to trace Alan and before long it was discovered that he was in prison in London for embezzlement, serving a five-year sentence. His real background came to light and his tales of what he had done in South America, including his story of being decorated were shown to pure romanticism; he had never left England.

BACK IN the bosom of her family, Marion was divorced from Alan in due course and might have resumed her studies had war not broken out and she felt that she should make her contribution helping as a nursing auxiliary in military hospitals. There she met and married, after a whirlwind wartime romance, Captain Gordon Farquhar of the Argyll and Sutherland Highlanders, Adjutant to Colonel Marsh.

Marion, near to tears, concluded her story. "I loved Gordon so much but we had such a short time together. We married in a little village called Auchiltibuie overlooking the beautiful Summer Isles off the west coast of Scotland when he was on leave and we honeymooned in the Summer Isles Hotel. When Gordon died I came to live on the estate, where my sister, Joan, was living with her husband Peter. Colonel Marsh gave me a job. The only shadow over my period on the estate is that Alan got in touch again, trying to blackmail me. Colonel Marsh dealt with him but I don't have any details, I just know that he stopped bothering me. But with Gordon I had experienced the best that life can possibly give me. I didn't think it could ever get any better than what I had with him but I resolved to enjoy the good things that came my way and I think, Andrew, that you are good but I have also been badly hurt and, as I said once before, I will never hurt anyone deliberately. That is why, Andrew, my wish and desire is for you and I to enjoy one another as we have done but in no way to hurt Kirsty and the boys. I don't know if I can do it, it will take much dedication and resolve in our parts but I would like to try. Would you try, Andrew?"

By now the restaurant was empty except for the ever-attentive waiter still on duty at the far end of the room. They rose from the table, slightly shakily from the wine, and both emotionally drained. After Andrew had rewarded the waiter for his patience, they went to Marion's cabin.

Chapter 11
Across America

The *Mauretania* arrived in New York just under five days after leaving Southampton, not her speediest crossing but commendable since she averaged over twenty-four knots, no mean achievement for a liner, which by then was twenty-five years' old. During her life she gained a reputation throughout the world for her speed, reliability and her ability to work hard. At one stage in her career she crossed the Atlantic eighty-eight times over three years without a rest, an achievement seldom, if ever, equalled by an ocean liner. In 1908 she took the Blue Riband of the Atlantic from the ill-fated *Lusitania* and for the next twenty years was the fastest liner in the world. She held many other records such as the fastest crossing over twenty-seven knots, a speed much in excess of that for which she was designed.

The crossing, which the *Mauretania* made when Marion and Andrew were passengers was not a record-breaking one but the time passed all too quickly for them. During those five days they had got to know one another well since – in addition to the revelation of her past on the evening of their White Star restaurant dinner – they had talked at length many times. They had not resolved the fundamental and very serious problem, which faced them concerning their relationship but it was now completely out in the open between them and they were able to face it. Andrew at one point light-heartedly compared their situation with that of the young Highland couple who left their wedding dance rather late in the evening to go to a lonely cottage far up the glen, where they were to spend their honeymoon. By the time they arrived it was Sunday and the young man had doubts as to whether he should consummate his marriage on the Sabbath. So uncertain was he that he left his bride and walked all the way back to the village, knocked up the minister and asked him whether it would be in order for him to do his duty. The minister thought long and hard before delivering his verdict, "Yes, it will be in order, provided you don't enjoy yourself!"

DISEMBARKATION COMPLETED, they booked into an hotel in Manhattan with the intention of having a couple of days sightseeing in New York, which they found to be a fascinating place, full of interest and with a surprise round every corner. Their hotel was not far from Times Square and as they stepped into the Square they had the feeling that they were at the centre of the world. They stood fascinated as they read the world's news displayed in moving lights on the New York Times building, with the kaleidoscope of people passing, people from every country in the world, people who were now Americans seeking the American Dream. Everything was so different, the policemen with their flat hats and guns on their hips, mostly with Irish accents and Irish names, the colourful taxis so different from the black London cabs, the huge sleek buses with their high windows and the overall buoyancy and friendliness of the people. Although the effects of the Great

Depression were still being felt, there was very little sign of it on the streets of New York.

Marion and Andrew did what nearly every tourist did, they went to the top of the recently built Empire State Building, the highest building in the world and marvelled first at the way the elaborate elevator system took people up and down and then at the unique view from the top. Visits to such places as Carnegie Hall and the burgeoning Rockefeller Centre complex were squeezed in, interspersed with visits to the stores in Broadway and some of the famous restaurants of Manhattan. Their last few hours were spent in Central Park, that oasis of greenery amidst so many massive buildings. Marion and Andrew had seen New York on the cinema screens back home but to be there, to see if for the first time – to look up at the skyscrapers, to see the Statue of Liberty, that symbol of all that is America towering over the Hudson River, the gateway to the United States – was an experience they knew they would never forget for the rest of their days.

As always their time was all too short and they entered the cavernous Grand Central Station to catch to train on the next stage of their journey. Grand Central epitomised America: it was big, shining, efficient, its population bustling and cosmopolitan. The centre of the railway system of the eastern seaboard of America, all railroads radiate from New York Grand Central Station. Andrew was again reminded of that Scottish lad from the countryside who took the train to Edinburgh on his first visit. When he arrived at Waverley Station he made his way to the station buffet, had a dram or two, something to eat and then fell in with some enjoyable company, so he drank in the station bar until it was time to catch his train home. When asked next day what he thought of Edinburgh he replied, "Man, it's a grand place, yon Edinburgh... it's a' covered in glass!" Andrew felt that Grand Central indeed was America!

The train journey to Denver was another experience not to be forgotten – nearly three days on a train! There was much to remember but perhaps the one noise, which they remembered most was the haunting wail of the locomotive whistle, particularly as it sounded at frequent intervals throughout the night, warning people that the train approached the many unguarded level crossings. The low pitched 'whoo-oo-woo' of the steam whistle coupled with the clickety-click of the wheels on the rails sounded as an overture to dreams as Andrew and Marion lay in one another's arms in their rolling, lurching couchette. During the day there was much to see in the brief intervals between eating huge meals in the dining car, big industrial cities, small country towns, vast prairie areas, farms large and small, magnificent rivers and panoramic views. When the train stopped at coaling and watering depots, the passengers had a chance to stretch their legs and to take a walk outside the station, for Andrew and Marion their first chance to see rural America and Americans at first hand.

THE UNION Pacific Transcontinental delivered them on time at midday in Denver where a reception party of Colonel Marsh's cousin and his family met them. At Marion's behest Andrew had donned his kilt for their arrival at Denver and there was a huge cheer from the welcoming party and the other people in the station as he stepped off the train. Saying 'hello' and 'welcome' to their guests from the old country took some time in the station concourse but eventually they were on their way, in a cavalcade of Buicks and Fords on the 80 miles or so to Last Chance.

Realising that their visitors would be tired after the long journey, the welcome dinner had been arranged for the following evening, so there was a chance for Andrew and Marion to meet and get to know the family. Colonel Marsh's cousin, Joan, was a second generation American lady who had married a man whose family could be traced back one hundred and fifty years to the War of Independence and who rejoiced in the typically American name of Wilbur Washington. Colonel Marsh's brother had immigrated in the early part of the nineteenth century to farm in the new lands of mid-America and had been successful, eventually acquiring the ranch adjoining the Washington's ranch. So when neighbours Wilbur and Joan married they were heirs to a considerable combined property. Both male parents were dead and the ranches had passed to Wilbur and Joan, while the dowager ladies lived separately in handsome houses that they had built for themselves on the ranch. Wilbur and Joan had two sons, one of whom was in oil in Texas and the other, Quentin, helped to run the ranch along with his sister, Wilma. Neither Quentin nor Wilma were married although Wilma had a partner named Justin who lived with her and who was ostensibly a script-writer for a film company. Quentin said cynically that he must be a ghost writer because nobody had ever seen his name on any credits!

Andrew and Marion enjoyed meeting them all, they were very friendly, except perhaps Justin who was rather aloof and slightly aggressive. They put this down to his being unsure of himself not being a full member of the family but wondered, from various things that were said whether he was thought of as living off Wilma who worked hard on the ranch. The next day was spent seeing round the extensive property and discussing the plans for Jeanokie when she arrived and the evening was spent eating. The 'welcome' dinner involved all the family including the 'grannies' and there was a steak barbeque set up in the courtyard of the ranch house, which opened on to huge areas of lawn on either side of the driveway, stretching seemingly miles to a boundary of beautiful poplar trees. It was a fine September evening but it was planned that after the steaks the company would retire to the conservatory, as it tended to get rather chilling as sundown approached. Although the two visitors were becoming used to American eating, in New York and on the train, they were not prepared for what faced them that night. The steaks were as enormous as they were delicious; likewise, the wines, sauces and salads, which accompanied them. Most of the company took a stroll across the lawns to the gardens at the side of the ranch before resuming eating the delectable sweets and drinking the delicious coffee so favoured by the Americans.

The evening had a very happy family atmosphere and by the end of it, both Andrew and Marion felt very much at home. Marion knew her hostess's mother from the time she came to visit her brother-in-law Colonel Marsh when she did her European tour after her husband's death and got on very well with her. Even Justin was more amenable than he had been on the previous evening so they went to their beds content that their stay in Last Chance would be a pleasant and successful one. Tomorrow their work would start in earnest.

Chapter 12
Last Chance ranch

After three days familiarising himself with the workings of the ranch, Andrew prepared to take the train back east again to meet Hugh and Jeanokie at Chicago. This time he was taking the more northerly line down the River Platte valley to Omaha and so through to Lake Michigan and the great, busy, bustling and in many ways the bad, city of Chicago. After twelve years of Prohibition in the United States, Chicago was one of the main centres for liquor running on the eastern seaboard and had attracted more than its fair share of gangs and hoodlums. Despite Prohibition many people wanted drink and were prepared to pay handsomely for illegal stuff. Besides, the hoodlums were prepared to go to any lengths to be in a position to supply this profitable market with the result that gang warfare, murder on the streets, bribery of officials and suchlike were common. The authorities, thanks to the efforts of the famous Federal Bureau of Investigation under its equally famous leader, J Edgar Hoover, were getting things under control and many of the gang leaders and the behind-the-scenes people who organised and financed the illegal activities were being convicted and put behind bars.

Still, Chicago was a big and important city, the second biggest in the United States, an important seaport and the focal point of most of the railway systems in the north of the country. Vast quantities of material came into the country and were exported through its extensive harbour facilities and wide ranges of goods were manufactured in its huge factories. It was especially well placed to export vast quantities of grain and cattle from its rich agricultural hinterland. It was into this vast teeming city that Andrew arrived to await the arrival of the steamship *Alcantara* with Jeanokie and Hugh, her groom. He found himself a comfortable hotel not far from the city centre and after checking with the shipping office he realised that he had a few days to wait before the *Alcantara* arrived.

While at Last Chance he had kitted himself with clothes so that he looked like the average 'yank' and was thus able to wander about without looking in any way conspicuous. This was a deliberate policy, stemming from what he had heard about Chicago but he need not have bothered because he never encountered bullets flying about the streets or big cars with men standing on the running boards firing tommy-guns. Instead he was made quite welcome by everyone he met and most people seemed delighted to meet someone from Scotland and they all wanted to know if he knew Harry Lauder, the Scottish music hall and vaudeville theatre singer and comedian, who was a great favourite with most Americans. In fact, Andrew wondered whether, if he had worn his kilt he would ever had to pay for anything, which he certainly wouldn't if he had been willing to sing 'Roamin' in the Gloamin'!'

With no bars open and not wanting to get involved with the bootleggers (although that would have been easy enough) he became addicted, like most Americans, to drinking coffee, strong and in vast quantities. The only work he had to do was to organise the horsebox for Jeanokie on the trip to Denver.

When the *Alcantara* arrived in nearby Milwaukee he was permitted to go aboard and found both Jeanokie and Hugh in good order, both having seemingly enjoyed the leisurely crossing. She was a steady ship and the weather had been moderate so neither suffered from the usual shipboard illness. Hugh had got on well with the crew and his few fellow-passengers and he had received plenty volunteer help with looking after Jeanokie, a favourite with many of the crew. There had been no suspicious incidents to cause any anxiety for Hugh.

It was an anxious few minutes now though for both Andrew and Hugh as they watched their charge being slung from a huge crane and hoisted on to dry land but Jeanokie bothered not, it was just another experience for her, or so it seemed. Then into her horse box, which provided horse and man to travel in considerable luxury – a padded stall designed so that she could stand or lie and yet was restrained from being thrown about with train movements, such as occurred during shunting. At one end was a comfortable cabin for Hugh, equipped for the day and night travel while at the other end was a store for hay and concentrate feed. The wagon had its own water supply for man and horse and since they were travelling attached to a passenger train the men fed in the dining car. The journey was again uneventful and although Andrew was now a seasoned American train traveller it was all a great thrill for Hugh, his first time outside England.

The last part of the long journey, from Denver to the ranch, was by road and the joy of Jeanokie knew no bounds when at last she stood on grass again and was reunited with Marion. When she was released into her paddock she ran and ran for sheer joy! She was going to like America! Her American hosts liked her too, they thought she was a superb horse, of outstanding appearance and wonderful temperament and both Wilbur and Joan shared Colonel Marsh's opinion that she was a potential winner. As soon as she had settled down Wilbur rode her and was very impressed with her condition and performance after such a long journey.

The ranch and its visitors soon settled to a routine, with the training of Jeanokie the topmost priority. In the wide open spaces of the ranch she was working most of the day, being ridden by one or other of the team and loving every minute of it. The aim of the programme was to get her muscles hardened up and to this end she was walked for up to ten miles a day, with occasional short sprints, just long enough to verge on making her sweat. They wanted her to reach a high level of fitness without being seen by prying eyes and there was no better place to do that than in the wide acres of Colorado. There was great excitement amongst the team when, even in a non-competitive situation, she achieved at a routine time trial a performance which exceeded their wildest dreams. Work was mixed with pleasure and there were days, in the pleasant late fall weather when groups of them from the ranch went on day-long rides to the mountains, taking with them food for the day. In the late autumn the colours of the leaves were superb, and from the higher ground it seemed in places that the very earth itself had been painted in that beautiful natural yellow colour, which verges on russet in certain lights.

On these occasions Andrew and Marion were never alone, as indeed they were never alone during their time at the ranch. Their hostess, totally unaware of any relationship between them had naturally given them one of the elegant guest rooms each. Andrew and Marion, adhering to their resolve to keep their affair strictly between themselves and not to let it impinge on others in any way carried on as though they were strictly two business acquaintances. It was in reality an amazing demonstration of self-control by the pair of them and especially by Marion who set the standards. They had concealed their affair back in England but there they were only working together whereas here they were living in the same house, in almost adjacent bedrooms and never once did they transgress. It was almost as if Marion, the arch organiser, knew that she would be able to surreptitiously arrange the moment, as she had done in the case of the London trip and of course during the sea-voyage.

THE OPPORTUNITY came when their hosts suggested that they should take a few days' vacation to see some of the wonders of Colorado State, in particular the Grand Canyon, the Rockies and perhaps even Las Vegas. Conscious of the fact that Colonel Marsh was financing the journey to America, Andrew was at first hesitant but Wilbur insisted, arguing that while they may have been thoroughly enjoying their work with Jeanokie on the ranch they had been working very long hours and were entitled to a break. He also assured them that he would tell his cousin that he had offered the break, telling a little white lie that their health was suffering and giving the hosts some concern! Wilbur organised a large station wagon for them and off they set on their trip, Marion driving because she had volunteered to tackle the hazards of the left-hand roads.

It was a dream holiday in the vast spaces of the west and especially in the Rocky Mountains. Part of the area had been declared a National Park by the government in 1919 so there were good facilities for tourists and ample opportunities to visit many of the attractions even if they had only a short time available to them, as was the case with Andrew and Marion. They had been well warned by Wilbur and Joan to be aware of the huge distances involved in America as compared with Britain. They had learned, for example, that the Colorado River flows through the Grand Canyon for nearly two hundred and eighty miles, the distance from Newcastle to London. To people accustomed to thinking that the Corrieshalloch Gorge in the Highlands of Scotland or the Avon Gorge in Bristol were big, then the American equivalents appear immense. In the week available to them they covered over three thousand miles. They were tempted to visit Las Vegas, the famous gambling city in the desert, but Andrew's Calvinistic past intervened and, more significantly, lack of time made such a visit impracticable. Nothing else was missed however, although the pace was hectic and relieved by very pleasant evenings and enjoyable nights. As tourists they made use of the relatively new concept of 'motels', usually very good quality roadside hotels, which provided a self-contained room and separate dining facilities. Many of these were located at places where there was a sightseeing feature or a fabulous view and in one such motel on the plateau they were lucky enough to see one of the fairly rare phenomenona of that area, caused by the massive Rocky Range. Under certain weather conditions the atmosphere can be so clear that from the height of the plateau there is an extensive and clear view over the plains and deserts to the very distant horizon. Occasionally, as happened for the benefit of Andrew and Marion, or so they thought, a thunderstorm can roll in at great height, hoisted by the mountain range and precipitate rain in great quantities, visible to a watcher in the mountains. The phenomenon is that the rain does not reach the earth; it is evaporated by the rising, earth-heated air and swept back into the heavens. The phenomenon lasts only a short time and seeing it depends so much on the position of the sun to illuminate the rain particles that the gods must have been looking favourably on Andrew and Marion that day. It was the highlight of their holiday and a sight that was to remain with them in their minds, along with such sights as the phosphorescence in the wake of the *Mauretania* forever.

That day was more memorable because they stayed at an hotel called Heaven, so called, it is believed because it was very close to Heaven! It was high up in the mountains, on a ledge with a panoramic view to the west. All the rooms were arranged so that they could be used curtainless and had huge windows through which sunsets, often magnificent, could be viewed. By now the pair was well accustomed to the American level of eating and both could do justice to the huge steaks set in front of them. Andrew on one occasion remarked jocularly that all the American chefs did by way of butchering a beef steer was to take off its horns and wipe its bottom before they cooked it and put on a plate! A fair comment and sometimes it seemed not too far from the truth. They were also accustomed to the 'dry' meals, with fruit juices or equivalent the only liquid. Very occasionally, usually when the head waiter or suchlike of Scottish extraction had a blether with Andrew about the old country, they would be offered one of the hotel's 'speciality fruit wines' with their meal. This was presumably after the chat with Andrew had assured the hotel people that he was not an undercover agent! Andrew and Marion appreciated the fact that apparently in America barley can be classified as a 'fruit' when appropriate! The quality was perhaps not that of a Macallan whisky but it complemented a perfect meal in a perfect hotel with perfect rooms, perfect views, and even a perfect sunset laid on especially for them.

However, Andrew and Marion had other things on their minds besides sunsets. As they lay on the hotel's luxurious bed, relaxed after they had consummated a memorable day, they talked once again of their future, which they had hardly had an opportunity to do since that unforgettable evening on the *Mauretania*. It was clear that Marion was wavering in her resolve about not causing hurt and it was Andrew who had to gently remind her of what might happen if they failed to maintain the standards they had set for themselves over their affair. Yet they both knew that they were growing even closer to one another and that probably sooner rather than later one or the other of them would make the total demand on the other. So far fortune had favoured them in their secret relationship and they had been able to live effectively as man and wife for short periods, although between those periods they had to work hard at maintaining the pretence. In the end they reached no definite conclusion – they would continue with their 'wait and see' policy.

Their short holiday over, they returned to Last Chance to be told that Colonel Marsh had telegraphed his full support of the holiday idea but had indicated that now that Jeanokie was settled and all the necessary plans laid for her training, he would like them to return a little sooner than planned because there had been certain developments at home and he needed their help.

Chapter 13
A strange American seems to know the secret

It was a wrench for Marion and Andrew to leave the relaxed and pleasant life at Last Chance Ranch. Everybody had been so kind to them and made them very welcome so that they were almost part of the family. They had been very circumspect about their relationship; they had lived under the same roof with bedrooms in close proximity but had never, however difficult it was at times, allowed their relationship to show. If anyone of the family suspected that they were in love with one another, they gave no sign.

Jeanokie by this time had completely settled to life on the ranch and she, and Hugh were inseparable. There was no attempt to conceal true feeling there – she adored Hugh even more than Andrew and Andrew had no scruples about leaving her in America for a little longer. She had grown physically hard, thanks to a rigorous training programme and her endurance had improved beyond all measure. Hugh had taken in a big way to the American life, so much so that Andrew wondered whether he would ever settle down back home.

The journey home was uneventful except for a disturbing incident, which befell Andrew in Long Island. They had three days between arriving in New York and the sailing of the *Mauretania* and they spent these with friends of the Washingtons, who had a holiday home near Flushing on Long Island. Here in contrast with life on the ranch, Marion and Andrew had the sea literally at their doorstep, or at least at the end of a short path down to the shore. On the private and secluded beach, they had at their disposal a jetty and a thirty-foot yacht. Neither of them were accomplished sailors but with some instruction and in the calm weather they were able to sail her on her engine along the coast. Their hosts had to travel into the city daily so they had most of the day to themselves to walk on the beach, to laze about on the yacht and to make love, making up for the time it was not possible on the ranch. It was into October and the weather was barely suitable for swimming but they even managed that on a few occasions. Time was too short to meet many people but on the last evening they were guests of honour amongst a host of neighbours and friends at a dinner party in their host's home. Although it was completely out of season and because they were not likely to be back in November, they were treated to an all-American Thanksgiving Day Dinner of corn-on-the-cob with maple syrup, turkey with cranberry sauce and pancake waffles and ice-cream, a memorable meal for their last evening in the States.

WHEN THEY were taking the air in the garden on that late autumn evening, Andrew was led aside by a large gentleman who could best be described as a 'typical American tycoon', a huge cigar belching smoke, whisky glass in hand, full of bonhomie. He introduced himself as Edgar J Curtis and confided to Andrew that he was a good friend of Justin at Last Chance. He claimed that he knew the outline of the story of why Jeanokie was in America and confided to Andrew that he had offered to take a sizeable financial interest in the horse and Colonel Marsh was at that very moment considering the offer. Andrew was flabbergasted and had no idea how to handle this development. At no time, back at the ranch, with his hosts, the Washingtons, or in letters from back home had there been any mention of any outside interest in Jeanokie. He fell back on the old army ploy of being stupid and ignorant, talking a lot about Jeanokie but saying absolutely nothing of significance, promising the earth but giving away not one grain of soil. While he was talking inconsequentially, his mind was working very fast and he was immediately suspicious of the fact that this man Curtis had mentioned the name Justin as his link with Last Chance. It ran through Andrew's mind that of all the people at Last Chance, Justin was the one with whom he had not been comfortable. As a guest of Colonel Marsh's family at Last Chance, he had to treat Justin as he did the rest of the family but he was always aware that Justin was somehow not quite one of the family. At the time, he had put this down to the fact that Justin had not been married to Wilma but with this strange development, Andrew started thinking there might be other reasons.

When a suitable chance came he broke off from Edgar J and sought out Marion. When told the story she too could hardly believe it and they decided to talk it over with their hosts after the guests had gone. They too were at a loss to understand the situation. Edgar J Curtis, it transpired was an acquaintance of a good friend and neighbour of theirs in New York, who happened to be on Long Island. They had no idea he had connections with Last Chance. A phone call to Last Chance deepened the mystery because the name Curtis was unknown to them! When it was made clear to the Washingtons that Wilma's partner Justin was involved, there was some hesitation and finally it was suggested that nothing more be said or done in America about the approach to Andrew but that Colonel Marsh be advised of the development by telephone as soon as possible.

As soon as all the guests had departed, a call was put through to Colonel Marsh and he was acquainted with this surprise development. He agreed that Andrew had reacted very correctly by giving nothing away to this man about Jeanokie and appreciated being instantly told. He would start enquiries immediately and advise Andrew and Marion of developments immediately on their return. Farewells were said and the next day the journey home started, with much quiet worrying about what forces were at work, apparently against their horse Jeanokie.

ANDREW AND Marion were met, a little to their surprise, at Southampton docks by Colonel Marsh and Peter who came aboard as soon as the *Mauretania* docked. Over a last drink before disembarking, the Colonel said he had come down to Southampton to have a private talk with Andrew and to discuss amongst them all the developments on the Jeanokie front. Andrew insisted that he would prefer to have the news given openly and the Colonel said that three days ago Kirsty had decided to go back to Scotland, taking the boys with her. It seemed that she just couldn't settle, however nice her house, however comfortable her life and however hard people tried to make her feel at home. It seemed that she had given no indication that she suspected anything between Andrew and Marion or anyone else, she was simply homesick for Scotland.

Andrew's reaction was of both sadness and relief with the latter most dominant. The four of them discussed the situation briefly, realising that there was nothing that had to be or could be done immediately. Andrew and Marion then waited anxiously to hear the Colonel's news, which was that he had reason to believe that an old enemy of his, a bad and wicked man, was behind the recent affairs concerning Jeanokie. This man had committed a terrible crime involving a prisoner-of-war, had laid a false trail to indicate that he had died but had in fact disappeared and Colonel Marsh had been given the task of hunting him down. Colonel Marsh had brought him to court in Germany and he had been sentenced to death. The sentence had been commuted to life imprisonment and the former German officer had been released in 1930 and had sworn revenge on Colonel Marsh.

There was no time for more than the briefest outline of this story and there had been less chance for Andrew to bring the Colonel up-to-date with the news from America. Colonel Marsh decided that they should stop overnight at an hotel and catch up with all the news over dinner; he accordingly booked his party into the appropriately name Nag's Head at Kings Worth, on the road home from Southampton. In the comfortable, relaxed and very English atmosphere of the Nag's Head, over an excellent dinner, each brought the others up-to-date with their stories. The Colonel was already familiar with Jeanokie's progress and had been briefly apprised of the Edgar J incident and when Andrew gave him details of the encounter, he simply and significantly said, "That makes sense."

But the story they all waited to hear was Colonel Marsh's one about his sworn enemy, a story that intrigued them because none of them could imagine the Colonel having an enemy, let alone a deadly one. The story took them right past the coffee and almost to the end of a large bottle of Drambuie.

Chapter 14
The story of Colonel Marsh's enemy

Colonel Marsh, relaxed in a deep leather armchair, with a glass of Drambuie at one hand and a cup of coffee at the other began to tell his strange story to his attentive audience of Peter, Marion and Andrew. In his calm authoritative way, he said, "This terrible story, in which I am inextricably involved starts in the year 1917, in a prisoner-of-war camp for British soldiers in the outskirts of a town called Charleville-Mezieres in Northern France. Many of the prisoners-of-war were Jocks and to guard them was a detachment of German soldiers, mainly elderly men unfit for front-line duties and active-duty men recovering from wounds. Sergeant Hans Garstein, who was in day-to-day command of the camp was under Lieutenant Franz Shicklgruber. One day, the sergeant was supervising the sending out of prisoners from the camp to work on various farms in the area to help feed the German war machine. On this fatal day Lieutenant Shicklgruber was feeling terrible. His head was throbbing like a Sultzer diesel engine under load, his stomach was heaving like a tramp steamer in a gale in the Baltic

Sea and his balance was suspect so that he waved like a palm tree in a hurricane. His temper was foul, he had already had his batman put on a charge for failing to undo a sleeve button of his shirt when he had laid it out. No German officer should have to undergo the indignity of interrupting his dressing to struggle to undo a button. The cause of his ill humour was drink. At a mess party to celebrate a fellow officer's birthday, Lieutenant Shicklgruber had become rather objectionable. He was not a particular friend of the birthday officer and when the party set off to go to the friend's house, he had not been invited. So he went off to a club in town on his own, drank heavily there but found no good company so his next stop was a brothel favoured by the officer class. There, because of his condition he did not perform well, got rather angry and made rather a fool of himself. When on his way out he heard a few of the girls laughing at some little joke of their own, he was convinced that they were laughing at him and he made a terrible scene. He was remonstrating forcibly and very rudely with Madame in the foyer when who should appear but the Camp Commandant Major Beigbeder. He tried to bluster but was curtly told to remember that he was a German officer, ordered to leave immediately and invited to attend at Major Beigbeder's office at oh-seven-hundred hours the next morning.

"To get up early after such heavy drinking took a great effort; to deal with his batman for the heinous crime of leaving a button unfastened and to face his senior officer took him to the limit of his endurance. The fact that the Major had also been in the brothel meant that Lieutenant Shicklgruber would be dealt with privately but this did not mean lightly. During the interview, he was left in no doubt that his behaviour was a disgrace to the German Army and to the officer class in particular. The Major added that it was no surprise to him since Shicklgruber was not of the genuine German office class but merely carried a wartime commission. This condemnation deeply humiliated Shicklgruber and when the time came for him to take the morning appel, the military formation, he was seething and in very black humour.

"Private Sandy MacKay of the 4th Battalion, the Black Watch had been taken prisoner in no-man's land when he was a member of a party of stretcher bearers who were attempting to recover two wounded men from a shell-hole. Unfortunately, the Germans had heard the moaning from the shell-hole and, unsure whether the noises came from Germans or Britishers, they had also sent out a rescue patrol. Private MacKay was acting as forward sentry for the British party. They had the casualties on stretchers and were about to return to their trenches when Sandy saw the Germans and to create a diversion he crawled to the next shell-hole and started to moan and cry out, pretending to be injured. By the time the Germans located him and took him prisoner his own party had reached safety. For his quick thinking and taking the risk of being shot he was awarded the Military Medal. Private MacKay was a very ordinary soldier, no hero really, he simply did what he thought was the best thing at the time. Two attributes he had, however, were a sense of humour and a sense of the ridiculous, both of which had often helped him get through the trials and

That morning in the prisoner-of-war camp at the Charleville-Mezieres these attributes were the death of Sandy MacKay.

"Standing in their lines at roll-call, the prisoners witnessed Lieutenant Shicklgruber weaving his unsteady way across the parade ground obviously doing his best to maintain military bearing and equally obviously having the greatest difficulty doing so. As he approached Sergeant Garstein to accept the parade he stumbled and had to be helped back to the vertical by his sergeant. Sandy, realising the situation and enjoying the sight of a German officer disadvantaged said, not too quietly, to his mate standing next to him, "Christ, the bugger's pissed oot o'his fucking mind," and a titter ran round the ranks.

"The sergeant heard the remark, spotted the culprit and might have let it pass had not the officer also realised something was going on and demanded an explanation from the sergeant. Garstein realised his officer's bad humour and attempted to make light of the incident but to no avail and he had no option but to explain and name the man who made the remark. Being laughed at twice within a few hours was too much for him and Lieutenant Shicklgruber walked up to Private MacKay and struck him forcibly three times across the head, once on his throat, then on his face and finally on his temple with the heavy end of his swagger cane. Even the battle-hardened men of the parade, including Sergeant Garstein, were shocked and went to help Sandy, who had fallen to the ground, but were ordered to stand away by Shicklgruber who then ordered Sergeant Garstein to march the prisoners to their work. When many of them hesitated and made to help Sandy he called out the guard and in a few seconds the parade was facing a ring of German soldiers wielding rifles with fixed bayonets. The prisoners had no option but to march off leaving Private Sandy MacKay lying inert where he had fallen.

"It was fully half an hour before Sergeant Garstein obtained permission to attend to Sandy, by which time he was dead. Death was due to either a fractured windpipe or the blow on the temple or both but it was entered in the prisoner-of-war camp medical records as a heart attack while standing on parade. Those German soldiers who witnessed the violence were told that they had to accept the fact that, although they did not see it because of the speed of the attack, the prisoner had attempted to strike Lieutenant Shicklgruber who had simply acted in self defence.

"The prisoners were warned that if they wanted to survive to the end of the war they had best forget what they had seen. That very day Lieutenant Shicklgruber and Sergeant Garstein were posted to the Western Front on active duty. Over the next few weeks the thirty or so men who were on parade that day in Stalag 93 were transferred one by one to other camps and over the next few months, one by one they died. Before the end of the war they were either shot because they allegedly attempted to escape or because they stole food, operated radios or attacked German soldiers. All except Corporal Buchan of the Black Watch who had no chance to risk being shot for any of these fatal offences because he was put in the hands of the German medical authorities soon after the incident on the parade ground. He had been committed to a mental institution as a case of mental collapse, which was of interest to the German doctors dealing with similar cases amongst their own men. There were drugs that they wanted to test and they were not too keen to test them on their own men.

"Thankfully Corporal Buchan survived and when he was repatriated he was able to convince the authorities that he had very cleverly faked his mental illness. The British medical people worked hard to clear the drugs out of his system and he was able to report the incident in Stalag 93 to British Army intelligence officers. Before he was demobilised, he gave them the names of the Germans involved, the date of the incident and the names of most of the British soldiers who were prisoners of war in the camp at the time."

Colonel Marsh's audience, fascinated and horrified as they were by the story, were wondering what was the connection between a racehorse and an incident in a prisoner-of-war camp in 1917. He paused his story to charge his companion's glasses before apologising for having to explain his part in the story, not for his glorification, but merely so that the rest of the story would make sense.

Chapter 15
The story of Colonel Marsh's heroism

Seated comfortably in the residents' lounge of the Nag's Head in King's Worth, shocked and enthralled by the story of the happenings in Stalag 93, Andrew, Marion and Peter waited for the next stage in the story to unfold. As Colonel Marsh made to continue the story, Andrew interrupted his flow. "Excuse me interrupting you, Sir, but I'm sure it would be best if you told us the whole story, and at the same time tell us how you won your MC, something that you have never spoken about before. Then maybe that will explain your involvement in the POW business."

Colonel Marsh smiled, shrugged his shoulders in resignation and started on his own story.

"Before the war I was a regular soldier in charge of C Company Scots Greys based in the Redford Barracks in Edinburgh and on 5th August 1914 our Commanding Officer received his Top Secret orders to take us to France with the British Expeditionary Force. The army at that time was composed of 'Regulars' and 'Reservists', roughly in equal numbers and for both, going to war was a tremendous upheaval; the Regulars had to exchange the life of routine in barracks for life in the field and the Reservists had to leave home comforts for what they expected to be a sort of extended summer camp. Sadly, for too many it was anything but and the belief, prevalent at the time, that it would be 'all over by Christmas' soon proved to be false. At that early-stage mobilisation was very exact, precise, very secret and generally quite efficient. Orders to Commanding Officers contained typically cryptic military staff statements such as, 'Your company will de-train on platform 19 of Southampton Station at 11.47 pip emma'. The desk-bound planners had a field day, putting on paper their detailed plans for the mass movement of men and materials from their various depots to France. Little was overlooked, even to the extent of an order requesting officers to ensure that all mess-bills were settled before leaving quarters, presumably lest they were killed before they had time to send a cheque!

"C Company's journey to France started on the 13th August 1914 and the train journey to Southampton, the cross-channel passage and disembarkation in France went relatively smoothly, considering that we were part of an operation in which altogether about a hundred-thousand soldiers and their equipment were transported to France in the first wave, in about five days. Trains arrived at Southampton Docks at an average rate of fifty a day and ships sailed at a frequency of thirteen per day for Le Havre, Boulogne and Rouen. Regrettably, like the 'over by Christmas' idea, the light-hearted joke amongst the troops that they were heading for ruin (Rouen) proved prophetic for far too many of them. The whole operation was a credit to the Army staff who planned it and the civilian personnel who carried it out.

"C Company was attached to the 5th Division, part of Second Army Corps, which lined the canal running from Mons to

Conte. This canal was anything but a good defence position and presented no serious obstacle to troops who were determined to cross it, being on average sixty feet wide, never deeper than seven feet and crossed by about twenty bridges over its sixteen miles length.

"On both sides of the canal were houses, factories, slag heaps and other industrial paraphernalia, a built-up area, the sort of country in which no modern army had ever fought a war. On the right of the British Expeditionary Force was the French 5th Army and on the 21st August began the first major battle of the war, in an atmosphere of uncertainty and misconception, when the generals at the rear either did not receive information about what was happening on the ground and when they did, they did not believe what they were told.

The Royal Flying Corps were flying regular sorties over the German front and reporting troop movements, British and French cavalry pushed forward to probe and report on the enemy and prisoners were interrogated but the fog of uncertainty persisted amongst the commanders, French, British and German. In such circumstances the first set-piece battle of the war started on 23rd August 1914, both sides determined to advance but not really sure how they were going to do it. The Germans were working to the Schlieffen Plan, whereby they would make a big bold sweep through Belgium to the north of the French army, swing south to the west of Paris and pin the French against the back of their own defences, thus annihilating them. The rest of the front to the south towards Switzerland would remain static until the Germans, coming now from the west, would trap the French army and destroy it. To all intents and purposes the Germans regarded us, the British Expeditionary Force, as just part of the enemy forces, the German Kaiser describing it as a 'contemptible little army'. This arrogant remark gave rise to the proud title adopted by those who were amongst the first troops to land in France and who survived through to peace. They were proud to be known as 'The Old Contemptibles'.

"During the preliminary skirmishes to the battle, C Company cavalry was behind the forward line, available when required to go into the line as cavalry or dismounted as infantry. A squad of sappers reported to me that they had been ordered to lay charges at one of the major bridges over the canal. At the same time, I was ordered to provide an escort for them so I led a troop of my cavalry to the bridge, to find that the enemy had advanced to the other side of the canal and were digging themselves in to cover the bridge and prevent its destruction. While we were surveying the situation and deciding on a course of action, the sapper lieutenant explained to me how he intended to lay the charges on the support piers and the steelwork of the bridge; the canal had been narrowed by stone piers to about forty feet and a central stone pier built to support the ends of two lattice arch spans carrying a road and a railway. It was soon obvious that the Germans on the other side of the bridge held commanding positions because the slightest movement by our troops or sappers brought down a hail of small arms and machine gun fire. Something desperate had to be done so the sapper lieutenant and I devised a scheme, which we hoped would confuse the Hun.

"Next morning, under cover of pre-dawn darkness and aided by a mist over the canal waters, I led a hundred heavily armed men in total silence over the bridge. To ensure silence we swathed boots in strips of blankets, removed the buttons from our tunics and replaced them with string, covered our steel helmets with cloth and slipped sleeves hastily made from blankets over our rifles and bayonets. We reached the other side undetected and using the rope ladders we had brought along, climbed on to the roofs of the buildings in the sidings area of the railway and the warehouses alongside the canal. Most of the Germans seemed to be sleeping and we simply slit the throats of those we encountered before they could raise the alarm.

"By first light the sappers were ready to cross the bridge with their gear and in the eerie period betwixt dawn and day, when humans are at their lowest ebb unless keyed up, as we were, by the danger of their position, I fired a Very light, a flare gun, the pre-arranged signal that we were all in position. The Tommies in their hidden places held their fire as German heads appeared at the doors and windows and on-duty personnel went to check sentries. As soon as the first dead sentry was found the alarm was sounded and the area was swarming with Germans in various states of readiness, some even in various states of undress. My second pre-arranged signal sent a murderous hail of rifle fire, light machine gun fire and grenades into the enemy; the noise was deafening because our lads had taken a stock of harmless but noisy thunder flashes, which they threw from time to time to add to the confusion. The German commander lost all control of the situation for the first hour of the skirmish and pulled back his troops, during which time our sizeable reinforcements poured across the bridge to support us and took up positions in an ever-widening semicircle with its centre on the bridge-end. The sappers meantime were going about their business, preparing for the complete destruction of the bridge."

Here, Colonel Marsh broke off his story to explain how, in the wider world of the war, momentous decisions were being taken by the Army Commanders at General Headquarters on both sides, which were fortuitously of great help to him and his men. The French/British High Command decided to withdraw from the defensive line based on the canal and the Germans, in an unrelated move, decided to concentrate further to the north and, needing every soldier they could get, forbade a heavy counter-attack on the bridge salient, at least for that day. They moved the bulk of their army to the north to assist in the execution of the Schlieffen 'right hook', so Colonel Marsh and his men were left to harass the remaining German troops, pushing them slowly but firmly back throughout the day. In the early evening Colonel Marsh was called back to Divisional HQ where he was apprised of the wider situation, whereby the French/British forces were withdrawing to the west and south as a result of very severe setbacks further north, and it was vital that the bridge was blown as soon as possible.

Colonel March continued his story. "When I returned to the bridge, I decided to wait until night time then, before pulling out as silently as we arrived, to destroy the bridge. At 4 am, an hour before dawn, when the last soldier was safely across, the sapper lieutenant depressed the plunger to blow the bridge but nothing happened. The Germans were unaware of the failed attempt; they were still in their positions half-a-mile or so from the bridge, facing a non-existent enemy! The lieutenant volunteered to go forward and check why the charges had not gone off and to the repair the fault. He took with him his sapper sergeant but after an anxious half-hour wait, with the sky beginning to brighten, the sergeant returned, soaked to the skin to say that his lieutenant had slipped on the steelwork, fallen into the canal and as far as he knew had drowned before he had found and repaired the fault. I had hardly slept for two nights nevertheless I had no option but to go back on to the bridge to search for the fault, hoping that what I had learned from the lieutenant before the operation began would stand me in good stead. Despite his shocked state the sergeant insisted on coming with me and I was mightily relieved that he did. It was getting light before we were organised and we had to work our way monkey-like under the bridge, keeping out of sight. Suddenly a rifle shot rang out from the far bank and a bullet pinged off the steelwork of the bridge and this was followed by a fusillade of shots, with the bullets whining around us so that we had to press ourselves close to the beams of the bridge.

A patrol of Germans had worked their way towards the canal and, finding no opposition, had pressed right up the end of the bridge where an alert soldier had spotted us. The shooting alerted our lads who immediately set up a machine gun, rifle and mortar attack on the Germans, forcing them to seek cover. I guessed that by staying as high as possible under the roadway, we were out of the German line of fire as long as they were pinned down, so we worked our way like monkeys towards the central pier.

"At the pier there was no room for us between the top of the stonework and the underside of the bridge decking so we had to edge our way round the pier foundation, with barely a toehold on the slippery ledge. We had to spread-eagle ourselves against the stonework to find a finger-hold to steady ourselves and as we reached the quadrant facing the enemy we came under heavy fire. Because of the narrowness of the ledge we could move only slowly and we would have made a good target, spread-eagled as were, but thankfully we were almost perfectly camouflaged by our khaki against the stonework and this, along with the poor light and dawn mist, allowed us to reach the comparative safety of the steelwork. The sergeant spotted the fault; the multi-coloured cable had been used by a bird, perhaps a cormorant, as a perch and stretched it until it broke. The system had been wired so that all the explosives would go off simultaneously or, as had happened, not at all.

"Working in the shelter of a huge rolled steel joist, with an occasional well-aimed shot pinging off the other side of the web of the girder, we made good the broken wire and started the reverse journey. By this time the troops on both sides had begun to get organised and I saw heavier guns being brought up by the Germans. I knew then that time was short. It was too dangerous for us to scramble round the piers again because of the improving light so I decided to go up on the road and make a run for it. I had the bright idea of signalling back to our side by torch in Morse saying, "Job done – running home – need heavy cover – reply in Doric." I realised that the Germans would see the flashing light when my lads replied and knew the Doric would fool them. The reply when it came was simple, "Tin lizzie'll seen be comin' haf wye – loup ontil't – oor lads'll keep their bloody erses in the air till ye win' hame." Behind a barrage of everything our lads could throw across the bridge at the Germans, there came this rather primitive armoured car, a converted Bentley I think it was, reversing over the bridge, with its Lewis gun firing for all it was worth through a slit in the steel plating, which had been bolted round the car. As it reached us at the half-way pier it stopped, we leapt aboard and it made off, full speed ahead back to safety. The sergeant and I ran to the firing plunger to blow the bridge but was restrained by a major saying, "Hold on old boy, we'll get a few more of the buggers yet."

"He had given the order to stop firing as soon as the car was off the bridge and already there were signs that the Germans were preparing to cross. A German heavy lorry appeared on the bridge, with infantry sheltering behind and when they were about halfway, this major said very calmly, "Go ahead now, old boy!"

"I told the sapper sergeant that he should have the privilege and down went the plunger and up went the bridge. It was an awesome sight as the bridge sections lifted feet in the air, throwing the lorry and many German bodies up and into the canal. There was little time to gloat because we were already behind our flanking units as the British Expeditionary Force (BEF) started the great retreat from Mons. The demolition on the bridge doubtless held up the German advance for many hours, if not days, so it was all worthwhile."

Colonel Marsh shyly admitted that for his brilliant planning and execution of the bridge skirmish and for his bravery in crossing the bridge under fire to repair the broken cable, he was awarded the Military Cross and the sapper sergeant got the Military Medal.

By this time the hour was very late and Colonel Marsh concluded his tale by promising his audience that he would tell them the rest of the story as soon as possible. He promised to tell how, after the war, as a regular officer, he had been given the job of seeking out the perpetrator of a terrible crime committed by a German officer against a Scottish soldier prisoner-of-war, how he had accomplished the task but how, due to circumstances beyond his control, the matter was not yet ended.

As Marion, Andrew and Peter bade the Colonel goodnight, they were wondering to themselves what was the connection between a crime against a prisoner-of-war and a racehorse under training in America? It was several days before they found out and much longer before the matter was ended.

Chapter 16
The search for Schicklgruber begins

As the war wore on, Captain Marsh became Major Marsh but his active war was over in 1917, when he had a narrow escape from death when a German sniper's bullet grazed his skull, knocking him out and home to Blighty. Thankfully the permanent damage to his brain was minimal and in early 1918 he was back in France but this time at General Headquarters, on Field Marshall's staff. After the armistice in November 1918 he was posted to Aldershot and recommended to attend a selection course for Staff College. In January 1919, he was surprised to receive a summons from his CO, who told the now-Colonel Marsh that he was required to report to Brigadier Fortesque at the War Office in London the next day. Either his CO didn't know the reason for this unusual summons or wasn't telling him but Colonel Marsh had to wait until he was sitting, coffee in his hand, in the palatial office of the Brigadier before he found out.

He had been selected to lead a very delicate investigation into a reported war crime by a German Officer in a prisoner-of-war camp in France in 1917. A Scottish soldier, a POW, had allegedly been unjustifiably killed, his record of death falsified and a deliberate attempt made to eliminate all the prisoners who were witnesses, an attempt which had very nearly been successful. However, one prisoner-of-war, Corporal Buchan, had escaped being sent away because he was in the hands of the medical staff in their institution immediately after the incident took place as he had effectively pretended to be going mad. The medical people were trying to treat his 'madness' and were using a treatment of which they were doubtful and used him to test this treatment rather than their own German patients. Thus Corporal Buchan was able to report the happenings. He had been in a mental institution in Germany until the end of the war and had entered one in Britain after repatriation. The man's story was quite bizarre but the authorities here were very thorough and were prepared to believe him if some independent proof could be obtained. They were also aware that the story could spark off an international incident if it was not handled carefully. The War Office had decided that a man of senior, but not too high a rank, who had a proven record for fairness and understanding of people should make the initial discreet enquiries and the man chosen was Colonel Marsh.

Brigadier Fortesque explained that, as well as being relieved of all military duties, he could operate as a civilian. He was to be given an office attached to Whitehall, with clerical and research help. He would also have a field staff seconded to him for making enquiries, as required in Germany or elsewhere. He was given the name of a senior civilian police officer in Germany who knew the story and was authorised to cooperate with him and give every help in Germany. He was Detective Inspector Nabenquick and he and Colonel Marsh were to become firm friends during the course of the enquiry.

They were given a list of the names of British soldiers

believed to have been in Stalag 93 at the time of the alleged incident all of whom, with the exception of Corporal Buchan, were listed as having died at various other camps before the end of the war. He was also given clearance to talk to Corporal Buchan at the rehabilitation centre where he lived and he was determined to start his investigation there.

CORPORAL BUCHAN was smartly dressed in his best suit, obviously all spruced up for the visit of a senior officer, even one in civvies. He looked well, received his visitor courteously, talked as old soldiers do briefly about the war and when alone, with a pot of tea in front of them, Colonel Marsh invited the soldier to repeat his story in his own words. He deviated little from the story he had told originally but the Colonel learned that he, along with some of his pals, had been standing next to Sandy MacKay when he made his fatal comment and of course he had witnessed the actions of the German officer at very close quarters. At that point in the story Buchan's face turned very white, he buried his head in his hands and sobbed like a child. Between the sobs he kept muttering, "Yon face, yon bloody face, it was the face o' the deil himsel' – the mad bastard!"

When he had calmed down again he explained that the German officer's face haunted him. He remembered, all too clearly, wondering was he to be next but when Sandy dropped like a stone the Hun seemed satisfied, even scared. Buchan mentioned Sergeant Garstein almost kindly; he recognised that he might have been a decent man and one who certainly disapproved of his officer's actions. The rest of the story squared with the previously known facts and the Colonel left Buchan, convinced that he was perfectly sane and that the story was the absolute truth. His job now was to follow the trail of this German officer, Schicklgruber, and if he was still alive, to get him hanged, to avenge Private Sandy MacKay. This would also give Corporal Buchan peace and rid the world of an evil person.

THE COLONEL'S next step was to the War Office records department to check the names of the other prisoners who had died and to assemble his own list of where and when they had died. He then prepared for his first journey to Germany with the name of Sergeant Garstein very much to the fore of his mind. Where was he now, if he was still alive? If he were found, would he talk about the events of 1917? As well as the help of which he was assured, he would need the cooperation of the German military authorities and that was doubtful, so soon after the war. His main target was Shicklgruber and he started a file on him, in which he planned to record every single detail he could glean, from any source, from the day he was born, his friends (if he had any), his sources of income, his girlfriends, mistresses, wives, his hobbies and haunts, his schools, colleges and army units, his military history and so on.

Nabenquick's office was in Nardocstrasse, not far from the centre of Berlin, and when Colonel Marsh arrived after a difficult but interesting train and ferry journey from London, they quickly got down to work. Nabenquick was just over fifty years old, much older than Marsh, and had been a policeman since leaving school. He had spent three years in the Special Investigation Branch of the Feldjägercorps, the German equivalent of the British Military Police, when his job had been similar to the one to which he was now committed, dealing with officers and non-commissioned officers who abused their power in the course of their duty. He had already gathered much of the information Colonel Marsh required and they started their joint questioning at Shicklgruber's former schools. As expected he had been a loner, was unpopular with the other boys and exhibited himself as a bully. Despite these failings he had some ability as a leader, particularly at leading other people into trouble, from the consequences of which he usually managed to escape unscathed. His parents were good middle-class Germans, his father ran a successful printer's business and they lived in a nice suburb of Regensburg in Bayern, a pleasant town on the Danube. He had gone on to attend university but had been sent down because he had spent more time drinking and womanising than studying. His professor, who had counselled him on several occasions, saw in him a good brain competing against a doubtful, even evil, personality and the professor decided that the evil would prevail.

In the eyes of his family he was a failure and they withdrew support from him so rather than work for a living he saw the army as his salvation. The German Army in pre-first war days was very class ridden and, as the son of a mere master printer, he had few privileges accorded to him. However, when war came his talent for leadership earned him a commission and during the war his innate gift of self-preservation served him well and he rose rapidly in rank. A flesh wound at the end of 1916 took him to the German equivalent of Blighty, after which he was appointed to the prisoner-of-war camp at Charleville-Mezieres. According to German Army records his posting there was abruptly terminated and he was sent to the Western Front where he was reported missing, believed killed.

Sergeant Garstein was a regular soldier with an exemplary record until 1917. After a particularly arduous period in the front line he had been detached to serve in a military detention camp where deserters from the German army were dealt with and for several months he had been in charge of firing squads, an experience which had begun to affect him so that his CO had arranged for him to be posted to a prisoner-of-war camp for a spell. In late 1917 he had been accused of indiscipline and failure to obey an order and sentenced to ten years' hard labour but just before the armistice in 1918 he was shot and killed while attempting to climb the camp fence.

Colonel Marsh then meticulously checked the records of the prisoner-of-war camps to which the British soldiers who were on parade that fateful day had been sent, traced the German personnel of these camps and satisfied himself that the prisoners were all dead. With typical German thoroughness each death had been made to appear legitimate and witnessed by a German who was independent of the death. On interrogation some of the German staff said that they were aware of strange people being around but the regular staff had no contact with them and could certainly never identify them. Just one little clue resulted from days of searching records, tracing people and interviewing them in depth. One German ex-soldier remembered being in a beer kellar near the camp with another soldier, who was a stranger and when very drunk boasted of having got rid of an Englander that day. He had also remarked in his cups that he was fed up of the war and wanted to get back to his job in security in a steelworks in Essen. The only other detail that Colonel Marsh's informant could give was that he thought the stranger's regimental shoulder flash featured a fox.

With these insignificant bits of information, he started on the seemingly impossible task of tracing this witness, if indeed he had been privy to information about the illegal killing of a British prisoner-of-war. The only other person who could help to convict Shicklgruber, if he was alive and could be found, was Corporal Buchan.

Chapter 17
The wanderers are home

It was a disturbed homecoming for Andrew, to face the fact that his wife had left him and gone back to Scotland with the two boys, wondering as to the real reason for her action. People at the stables commiserated with him, saying how disappointing it was and how they had all hoped that she would settle down; not one single person gave any indication or knowledge of his relationship with Marion. As he thought it over again and again, Andrew marvelled that neither by thought, word, deed nor even look had they revealed their relationship to the many people with whom they worked and lived. His worry now was whether he could or should continue the deception and after much uncertainty, he was still unsure whether he should go and see his family in Scotland. There was so much to do now that he was home in Suffolk and back at work, planning the immediate future for Jeanokie as well as dealing with the day-do-day matters of the stables. Most importantly Colonel Marsh had to be 'debriefed' by him and Marion about the American trip and the strange events, which had taken place. The report was in many respects routine and already known to the Colonel – how well Jeanokie had survived the sea and rail journeys, how quickly she had taken to life on the ranch, and how she had accepted being looked after by Hugh. He was delighted to hear at first hand how her performance had improved and how well she looked. It was when Andrew came to talk in detail about the Long Island happenings that the frown came back to the Colonel's face. He recalled that he had not had time down in the hotel in King's Worth to tell them all about the German affair and promised that he would have his team up to the Hall for dinner one evening soon, when he would finish his tale. He told Andrew and Marion how, like the legendary Mounties, he had 'got his man' and had secured the conviction of a serious war crime of the German officer, who had been sentenced to death. However, the death sentence had been commuted to life imprisonment and after serving nine years he had been released in 1930 and was now 'the hunted turned hunter'.

THE GERMAN authorities had information that the officer had sworn revenge on Colonel Marsh, for having traced him and having him brought to justice. The police and other security authorities involved were unsure as to whether he would be acting on his own or whether he had enough money, power or influence to operate through hired agents. The information about the revenge vendetta had come from several of his fellow prison inmates; he had been quite open about his hatred of Colonel Marsh and boastful of his intention to harm him in any way that presented itself and to kill him if possible. Since his release Shicklgruber had disappeared, gone to ground, but the German police were keeping watch on his home and haunts. The news of the death of the racehorse in suspicious circumstances at Colonel Marsh's stables was the first thing to come to their notice which might be connected with Shicklgruber and then the mysterious man at Long Island heightened suspicion. At the same time there was the concern that these events might be totally unconnected with Shicklgruber but rather with a powerful racing syndicate which had for some time been under surveillance. This syndicate operated by manipulating a number of horses were often reared from very high quality stock but their breeding was not revealed and they were able to win races at good odds. For this method of working to be successful there was no room for opposition from 'unknown' horses, such as Jeanokie and it was possible that the horse, which had been poisoned had died instead of Jeanokie. There was not the slightest evidence of any of this; the business of producing a winning horse was not illegal, provided there was no substituting or misrepresentation. It was proving very difficult to trace the stable boy who had aroused suspicion at Colonel Marsh's stables – indeed he had committed no offence connected with the horses in the stables – the worst that could be said about him was that he was an unsavoury character with a bad temper and a bit of a con-man. Discreet enquires had been started through contacts in the FBI for American connections, but they were very busy chasing the liquor gangs and could only offer a watching brief.

Colonel Marsh had thought that Jeanokie was safe in America but the man in Long Island caused a great deal of concern. Was he working for the London syndicate or the German? Shicklgruber had never had any direct contact with Colonel Marsh but he was unscrupulous and in need of easy money and this led the Colonel to fear that he might attempt some form of blackmail or worse. The fact that Alan, Marion's first husband, was the London correspondent of the suspicious stable lad, Mick, only made the whole thing more unpleasant. With known connections in the shady London racing syndicate, Alan was just the sort of contact Shicklgruber might use to get at Colonel Marsh; putting the kibosh on Jeanokie's chances would serve both the syndicate's and the German war criminal's needs.

Chapter 18
The hunt is on again

Colonel Marsh felt he had to find Schicklgruber a second time. He had complete confidence in his German police contact, Detective Inspector Nabenquick, with whom he had developed a warm friendship over the years. He had the makings of a first-class team working for him to find Schicklgruber but still felt he needed a trusted aide nearby who was as determined as he was to 'get his man'. He had already come to hate this man Shicklgruber, a man whom he never met, a creature who had used his position to kill a helpless man and then gone to great lengths to conceal the crime, resulting in the deaths of many more innocent men – enemies maybe, but unarmed and defenceless. His actions had in all probability led to the death of one of his own side, Sergeant Garstein, who had fought honourably at the front but been falsely branded a criminal and shot solely because of what he knew.

To find Shicklgruber and get him dealt with was difficult. Colonel Marsh had very little to go on because of the ruthless and methodical way in which the Germans had covered up their tracks since he last hunted the criminal. He had Corporal Buchan, who would be the vital and only witness against Shicklgruber, and he was being quietly but carefully guarded lest someone decided that he couldn't talk if he was dead. He only had one slender lead from his first investigation, the drunken German soldier who had boasted in a beer kellar near the prisoner-of-war camp that he had helped to get rid of an 'Englander' who had insulted a German officer. This bit of information came from one of the many ex-German soldiers his team had interviewed and was vague. But the informant remembered the drunk saying in his cups that he was fed up with the war and wanted to get back to his job as a night-watchman in a steelworks in Essen. The informant seemed certain of this – he had thought at the time that a man who got very drunk and talked as he did in drink would not be very reliable as a watchman, of any sort.

Colonel Marsh felt as though he was going in wide circles, coming round to a place he had been years ago, when he had first brought Schicklgruber to justice. Despite his frustration, there was nothing for it but to conduct these two searches – first, or rather again, for the man in the beer kellar who spoke to the drunken officer who had worked before the war in a steelworks in Essen and secondly, a new informant, a driver for Stalag 93's neighbouring camp. Of the latter there was some official record, vague but possible and of the former – well, there were many steelworks in Essen and even more men! Of course one or both might be dead but even so, they both had army connections and the trail might be picked up from army records but there was little to go on.

Thinking on the problem, Colonel Marsh remembered the sapper sergeant who had helped him to blow up the bridge in northern France during the retreat from Mons. If he had survived the war, he might be just the sort of man to have on the team – he would almost certainly have the dedication to see the matter through. A hunt for him was started, a much easier hunt and within a month a report landed on Colonel Marsh's desk saying that he was working as a solicitor's clerk in a practice in Carlisle. He was Mr Norman Ruskin, married with two young sons and a very good reputation at his work and socially. Nothing had been said to him or his employers, of course, about the reason for the enquiries but the brief preliminary report concluded by saying that Mr Ruskin was wheelchair-bound, having lost both legs when a land mine exploded near the end of the war.

On the pretext of a sentimental journey looking up wartime acquaintances, he called on ex-Sapper Sergeant Ruskin, or rather ex-Regimental Sergeant Major Ruskin and enjoyed an old soldier's reunion. Afterwards Colonel Marsh called on the head of the firm of solicitors for whom Ruskin worked, got a first class testimonial and agreement that if Ruskin was willing to join the search team, leave of absence would be granted. Within a few weeks Norman Ruskin was installed in a ground floor office in the same building at Colonel Marsh and a huge pile of army records set in front of him. Another valuable member of the team, Gilbert, a Polish immigrant to Britain, had started the war as a batman but when it was discovered that he was a fluent German speaker he had been drafted into the intelligence corps and had spent most of the war interrogating prisoners. In fact, because of his central European accent he was often taken as a native German, particularly when dealing with less well educated Germans and this sometimes landed him in tricky situations! But it was useful in putting prisoners at ease and more ready to talk and sometimes give away useful information. He and Norman worked a lot together, becoming good friends and Gilbert soon became Norman's 'legs', handling the wheelchair and doing the legwork – they made a good and very useful team.

Within two months a 'new' informant had been traced, a

relatively easy task because he had been working in a neighbouring Stalag as a driver. He was Conrad Hoffman, a demobilised private who had already been interviewed by the German Military Police at the end of the war but whose official record of the interview had perhaps conveniently, been 'lost' and then 'found' again by Nabenquick. Colonel Marsh decided that it would be best if he were interviewed in the first instance by Gilbert in a quite informal way, on the pretext that the British team were trying to find a staff car which had disappeared from the Stalag at which he had been stationed at the end of the war. Hoffman had been warned never to talk about what happened the day he had suddenly and urgently been despatched with his utility vehicle to Stalag 93 but he was easily put at ease by the smooth-talking Gilbert. Naturally he was able to deny any knowledge of a stolen vehicle and when that threat of trouble was lifted, he was prepared to chat, almost boast about what he was ordered to do that day.

He recalled sensing an attitude of tension at camp reception, how two guards got into his cab with him and told him to drive to a certain hut where a body wrapped in canvas was loaded in the back. He then had to drive to a shop in the nearby village where an undertaker took charge of the body. Back at camp he was told to stay with his vehicle until required. From time to time that day he made runs to the local railway station with men from the camp, fully kitted as on a posting. No-one spoke and he collected replacement guards who arrived on various trains, all surprised at the sudden postings to the prisoner-of-war camp. Finally, he was ordered to drive three officers, a lieutenant and two captains to catch a train. Hoffman said he was certainly curious about what was happening but in view of the tension and the silence, he was convinced it was more than his life was worth to open his mouth. A strange day ended when he got back to his own camp to find that he was posted with immediate effect to join a company of troops heading to the front. He had often wondered what happened that day at that prisoner-of-war camp but he remembered the dire warning that he had received about talking about the events of the day and refrained from talking to anyone until now, when he thought it was safe and there was the hope of some reward for his information. He duly received his 'reward', soon after the interview with Gilbert he 'accidentally' fell in front of a train at a busy suburban station. The subsequent enquiry could establish no cause but those interested in the man believed he had either been cunningly pushed off the platform or had been threatened to the extent that he committed suicide. Colonel Marsh's feeling of sadness upon hearing the news of the death of this very important witness was only matched by his feelings of frustration. He pulled himself together and thought, "Blast it! I got you before and I'll get you again!"

Chapter 19
The POW murderer is captured

Colonel Marsh was sitting at his desk, puzzling over the details of the hunt for Schicklgruber, musing that Gilbert's interview with the dead informant Conrad Hoffman exactly matched that of ex-POW Corporal Buchan. The shrill sound of the telephone brought him back to the present with the good news from Detective Inspector Nabenquick to tell him that his behind the scenes research had paid off; he had heard that Shicklgruber had moved to Holland around 1930 but had not been heard of since. The German police contact also had a lead about a Dutchman, Jan Meyer, who ran a powerful racing syndicate in Holland and also had connections to the north-east of Scotland and London.

"There's that possible connection between Schicklgruber and Marion's nasty first husband again!" thought the Colonel before catching the end of DI Nabenquick's sentence.

"… and I'm going to the Netherlands to meet this Jan Meyer. If there's any significant news, I will let you know straight away!"

This conversation really had boosted the Colonel's morale and he went over to his drinks cabinet to pour himself a dram of the good stuff to celebrate. True to his word, a few days later Nabenquick calls the Colonel to give him an update of what he has discovered in Holland.

"Well, Colonel, I met the Dutchman, Meyer. He seems a very pleasant man and we had a good meal and a few beers canalside while he told me some potentially very interesting information. Jan confirmed his links with the north-east of Scotland, he told me that he owns a property there. He was able to buy this house because, acting for the Dutch Government, he was promoting the sale of bulbs from Holland… Are you still there Herr Colonel?"

Colonel Marsh had been concentrating so intently on what the detective inspector was saying that he had gone extremely quiet, sitting stock still, "Yes, yes Detective Inspector, it is all very fascinating, please do continue."

"Over the last few years, Mr Meyer got to know some of the locals and he often attended shooting parties near Cullokie called the Bogandreep Syndicate. He was invited to become a member of this syndicate and, wait, here is the really interesting news Colonel, he is due to attend a special dinner in Cullokie to celebrate the end of the shooting season in two weeks' time! Apparently it is the custom of the members to say thank you to their wives, partners and girlfriends by inviting them to this function and by all accounts it is always a most enjoyable evening to which friends can also be invited."

Nabenquick was getting more excited and starting to speak even more rapidly than he usually did, "Now because he was a member of the Bogandreep Syndicate, he asked if some members of his racing syndicate in Holland could come over to join in and enjoy the next dinner. The Scottish syndicate agreed and Jan told me that one of the people he had invited was a German. This man had only recently joined Jan's racing syndicate but seemed fascinated about the story of the racehorse that had been delivering milk at Blairmoss Farm. The German had been interested to know where the horse was now. Of course I told him nothing of my suspicions and did not mention the name Schicklgruber."

With the Colonel's mind racing, he came to the same conclusions as Nabenquick before he ended the call, "May I suggest, Colonel, that you and the police turn up 'unexpectedly' at this lovely dinner?"

Colonel Marsh agreed with Nabenquick and thanked him profusely for his valuable information and for his unfailing support. The next phone call he made was to his British police contacts, who had a photograph of Shicklgruber taken during the war with which they thought they would be able to identify him.

ALL THE arrangements had been made and the night of the dinner in Cullokie was soon upon them. The police were unobtrusively scattered around the Cullokie Village Hall while Colonel Marsh was hiding near the back exit. Inside the hall the guests – including the German, who was sitting with Jan Meyer and his other visitors – had finished the excellent main meal and coffees and wee drams were being served. The Secretary stood up to introduce the Chairman, who would give his customary speech. At this point the police decided to raid the dinner; they had seen Shicklgruber arrive and were able to identify him from the photograph. As they entered the hall, Shicklgruber, with his hunter's instinct, became suspicious and left his seat and made for the back door. As he rattled the handle on the back door, it opened and two British policemen made a grab for him from behind but he slipped from their grasp out in to the night. The Colonel, who was waiting outside, caught up with him and downed him with a magnificent rugby tackle. In a few seconds three men were on top of him and held him securely. He was handcuffed and leg cuffed and dragged roughly back to the doorway, obviously badly mauled. He was left there until a police vehicle arrived to take him into custody.

By now, everyone in the room had risen to their feet but the Chairman asked them all to resume their seats while he invited the Colonel to say a word of explanation. The rather dishevelled Colonel moved from the back of the hall to the stage to explain why the evening had been disturbed so unusually and suddenly.

When the Colonel had finished his explanation, he was given a round of applause for his story, for his prompt action and for having arranged for the police to be available. Suddenly once more the chairman was interrupted by a kerfuffle at the front entrance of the hall. The police were struggling to detain a well-dressed man who was shouting obscenities at them. The Colonel peered over the guests and could not believe his eyes. It was Alan, Marion's first husband and the man he suspected of murdering his horse Kilwinnock. He went over to the police and arranged for him to be handcuffed, ignoring the man's spiteful comments directed at him. Both the German and the Londoner had been a thorn in his side for many years and he was happy the hunt was over and that the was matter resolved.

Schicklgruber would not escape justice a second time and the Londoner could no longer harm Marion or Jeanokie. A rather silent and subdued audience then left the hall, thinking perhaps about Corporal Buchan, all the other prisoners and the people involved in the hunt for the wicked German officer. Jan, in particular, was shocked when he realised who Schicklgruber was and when it belatedly dawned on him that he had been used to find out about Colonel Marsh, as well as Jeanokie and her whereabouts.

Chapter 20
Jeanokie shows her powers

Colonel Marsh's return to his estate was a happy one. He informed everyone of what had happened in Cullokie. There were sighs of relief all round and not a few, if rare, tears from Marion. Andrew, Peter and Joan – who all knew of Alan's past treatment of Marion – were grimly pleased to hear of his arrest and comforted her with kind words but it was the Colonel who held her against his chest until she stopped crying. Of course they were also very relieved to hear that the Colonel had once again got his man, Schicklgruber.

With the arrest of the evil man Shicklgruber and the shady Alan Cox, life became more normal in the racehorse world. After the exciting event during the normally sedate event at Bogandreep Syndicate dinner, the usual enquiries were held and then the press interest died down both in Germany and in Britain. In the racing world, the trial of Shicklgruber was awaited with great interest by most people and the hope that it led to Corporal MacKay's death being avenged. In the Cullokie area, there was great praise for Colonel Marsh for his rugby tackle and for his organisation of the hunt for Shicklgruber and for the others who took part in it.

WITH PEACE, came a renewed sense of purpose as the team brought Hugh and Jeanokie back from America to her home stables in Newmarket. The mare was trained up and in top form but Hugh and Andrew decided that she needed a couple more months' training in England to make sure that she was up to form and for the recent controversy to die down. After two months of hard work by the whole stable, Colonel Marsh entered Jeanokie into a steeplechase race so that she could build up racing experience without attracting too much attention from the racing world too soon. The jockey was told not to race her too hard but she still came third.

Now it was time for the Colonel's dream of entering Jeanokie in the big races to come true. It was an exciting day when Jeanokie was scheduled to go to Goodwood to compete in the Ali Babi Festival Stakes due to be run at two o'clock with a moderately big and strong field. The going was specified as being good and the weather promised to be excellent. This last item of news especially pleased Marion because Andrew played a big part in training Jeanokie. Andrew was unable to get away from the stable due to a previous commitment but had insisted she should go because her presence would ensure that Jeanokie, who was extremely fond of her, would put on her best performance.

Indeed, when the race started, Jeanokie ran well and was up with the leading horses as they approached the finishing post but then she suddenly put on a spurt and shot ahead to win. The spectators were astounded, some smiling happily, others literally crying because their money had been on the other horse! There was a bit of chatter among the spectators because Jeanokie had really never been expected to win. Afterwards in the paddock, when Jeanokie's supporters had finished patting and praising her, she had a look on her face which said, "Well, what else did you expect from me!"

BACK AT the stable, Andrew was absolutely delighted and after they had phoned Blairmoss at Cullokie to tell him the good news, Colonel Marsh treated all those who had worked on Jeanokie to a quiet liquid lunch in the local pub.

But that day at Goodwood was just the beginning for Jeanokie and her team. When winter came, she appeared frequently back in Scotland at the Perth races. She became well known in racing circles and Colonel Marsh was very pleased indeed with her. Nonetheless, he still hankered for her to win in one of the country's famous races, particularly Ascot, the one in which all the newspapers featured the ladies with their stupid hats being blown about in the wind (the hats not the ladies)! Fortunately it was a calm day when they went to Ascot to see Jeanokie strive to become really famous. She obviously loved the atmosphere there, she was frisky and possibly amazed at how many people had turned out to see her. But in the race, she was up against some of the very best of the world's racehorses and try though she did, she failed to win. She managed second, which was a wonderful achievement. To get her name in the papers as a winner, even second, at Ascot pleased everyone except perhaps her owner Colonel Marsh, although he realised how well his efforts had been rewarded. So much so that he decided that, as much as she liked racing and the way she was treated by the race goers, she deserved and was due for retirement. At the stables, and everywhere she was known, people were very disappointed and some wondered if she wouldn't be happier to go back to Blairmoss and the milk round! The Colonel, however, was going to put her into a Retirement Home for Horses in Scotland where she would be very well looked after. She went up there and seemed very happy and had many visitors.

Chapter 21
Kirsty writes to Andrew

Kirsty was at home in Cullokie, to some extent settled but still worrying about how she had brought the boys back to Cullokie from Suffolk and away from the influence of Andrew, their Dad. She realised that she would never be able to settle in Suffolk missing her homeland too much.

She wrote to Andrew, not the usual letter but one in which she raised what was worrying her. The boys would soon reach the time for leaving school and starting work or making up their minds about their futures. As they were now placed, they would have to do this without the advice and influence of their father. She was aware that this situation was entirely due to her coming back to Cullokie and bringing them with her, despite the fact that they were quite happy and settled there in Suffolk. She herself was quite settled now, she had a job with Andrew's old pal in the grocer's shop and she was living in her old home but at times felt it was unfair of her after all he had done to give her a new life and a very comfortable home and so on. She was aware that he loved his new life as manager of a racing stable but maybe she hadn't given it long enough and now she was settled, she didn't really want to go back down south.

Andrew was shaken rigid when he got the letter. It made his situation, which was difficult enough as it was with Marion being always there and in his mind. But there was no doubt in his mind that he was very happy with his new situation – and pretty certain that it was not only because of Marion – and he would be very loath to give it up. As far as the boys were concerned he was thinking that they were perhaps old enough to make up their own minds. There was the alternative that they stay in one place and holiday in the other. Andrew said that once he heard the saying from Marion, 'However much you wanted a thing, it was best if you got it if nobody was hurt in the process'.

Another saying is also appropriate: 'Between the devil and the deep blue sea' but Andrew's solution was understandable – even if it meant continued concern.

Chapter 22
Back to a new normal

At Newmarket stables, Andrew was trying to get over his letter from Kirsty. He realised that she did not intend to come back to settle in the south and he was not inclined to give up the job he loved and Marion to go back north. After the good result at Goodwood when Jeanokie won her race – and her second placing at Ascot – he felt that his job was for life. After a great deal of thought, he wrote back and made it clear that the boys could operate the 'half and half' plan while they were still at school or after.

In the wider world of racing, the authorities took an interest in the other horse's death, rumoured to be in lieu of Jeanokie and their interest was making security more effective.

Colonel Marsh, relieved of his hunt for the man who had unlawfully killed Private MacKay in the prisoner-of-war camp in France, was able to concentrate on his stables, which were now a success thanks to the excellent staff he had gathered around him. Marion and Andrew had been very circumspect about their care for one another since their return from

America, difficult though it had been, but after the exchange of letters between Kirsty and Andrew they were less careful.

After a while Andrew learned from one of his friends in Cullokie that Kirsty and her new boss, his old pal, were very friendly and were thinking of setting up home together in the future. Andrew and Kirsty decided to divorce and they awaited the boys' decision. In the event, both boys decided to stay on at school in Cullokie and to visit their Dad in the holidays during which Andrew's older son, Jamie, could pursue his interest in becoming a jockey while Alex could learn more about horses as he wanted to be a vet. So Alex decided not to interrupt his schooling once again in Scotland as he wanted to achieve good exam results to enable him to go to university to be a vet. If Jamie really took to horse racing, then he could always move permanently down to Newmarket and the option was always open for Alex to join his brother.

Andrew, Kirsty and Marion were all happy with this arrangement. With the boys' school holidays imminent, Andrew and Marion agreed to wait until they had returned to Cullokie before they moved in together.

Marion and Andrew were quietly excited regarding the prospect of telling all of the people they cared for about their relationship and finally being open in their deep love for one another.

A *Mare's Tale* was originally drafted by Len Hall between 1995 and 1998, but remained incomplete until 2016 when Len decided to complete the manuscript ready for publication. When in school he was encouraged to use the Doric dialect of Scotland's North East, and this has been woven into the book.

About the author

Len, aged 18

LEN WAS born December 1925 in Ellon, sixteen miles North of Aberdeen on the River Ythan. The family moved to Aberdeen in 1927 and Len attended Mile End School followed by Robert Gordon's College. A cadet in the 102 Squadron of the Air Training Corp (ATC), he went on to study engineering, at Aberdeen University.

During WW2 and the in the middle of his second year at university he volunteered for flying training and attended the RAF's Initial Training Wing (ITW) flying Tiger Moths, at the time the early training aeroplane. He went to a holding unit at Heaton Park in Manchester before embarking the troopship *Alcantara* to America for flight training. He returned to the UK on the *Queen Mary* which was ferrying American troops home, and learned to fly Harvard twin-seat training aircraft. During this training made a landing too far up the runway, stopping dangerously close to the boundary fence. The other pilots nicknamed him 'Overshoot Hall' after that.

Just as the war was ending and within sight of his coveted 'wings', the Air Ministry said 'no more flying' without signing on for three years on a short service commission. He didn't want to forego the chance of completing his degree, so after the war ended he decided to seek demobilisation in time to get back to studies before the beginning of the academic year.

After his graduation when he gained his BSc (Eng), he worked as an engineer for many years in England, Wales and Scotland and finished working for the Scottish Agricultural Industries (SAI), a subsidiary of Imperial Chemical Industries (ICI).

He and his wife, Doris, who originally came from Wigan and was in the Auxiliary Territorial Service (ATS), had three girls for family.

They lived in Deskford, Moray, for a number of years where Len became involved in community life. He was Chairman of the flower show and the Community Council.

On retirement he taught engineering subjects (maths and physics) at Moray College in Elgin to civilian students and RAFservicemen from the military bases at Lossiemouth and Kinloss.

Len, 2016

He now lives in Fochabers, Moray.